Drop Dead Art

Andy Greensfelder

For Lynda + Richard
Great prior/new friends
+ wonderful hosts.

Love,
Andy

ISBN 1-4392-2864-7
EAN 13 : 978-1439228647

To order additional copies, please contact us.
BookSurge
www.booksurge.com
1-866-308-6235
orders@booksurge.com

I

Returning from a two-week vacation Wendel opened the front door and discovered a corpse. The stench of decay drove him two steps back, almost off the porch. When he took a second look even a computer programmer could see that Handler, his friend, had been shot in the head. He reached for his cell phone, and realized he hadn't taken it to Paris, so he stepped over the body and a dry patch of blood to call 911.

"Hello, Mr. Wendel. What's the problem this evening," the operator said. 911 had him on a list of repeaters, from calls about harassment by his neighbors.

"A murder."

"No kidding?" She sounded like he had said a cat was stuck in a tree.

"I just got back from vacation and discovered my house sitter dead in the front hall."

After a pause, she said, "You're not joking?

"No."

"Or exaggerating?"

"No, dammit."

While he waited for the police, he opened every window, disturbing dust that his once-a-month lovable cleaning woman hadn't bothered for years. Both doors to the patio were unlocked, which was how he left them when he was in town but was surprised to find them open after a two-week vacation. Maybe Handler had gotten into the same habit, or maybe the killer had broken in and left the doors open.

Perched on the front steps, he waited, trembling over the image of his friend. Two weeks earlier they had chatted over croissants and espressos in a Parisian cafe, before Handler had flown to LA, leaving Wendel to share the apartment with Handler's wife. Wendel gripped his fists and shook his head in disbelief that Handler was dead after expressing so much delight with his life. The memory of the croissant tasted sour.

"Jesus Christ, Wendel," said Chief Pruett as he ambled up the front walk. "What've you done now?"

Wendel swallowed his first reaction and pointed toward the door. He was in no mood for the Chief's smart-ass comments, which he appreciated when they tempered the smoldering neighborhood clashes.

"Meet Wendel," the Chief said to two LA County detectives whom he introduced. "Wendel has no first name." Although the Chief was a retired homicide detective and was more than competent to handle a crime scene, he explained that his one-man department in the village wasn't equipped for a murder without support. When the Council had hired him, Wendel and some of the others had been concerned that back in New York he had shot and killed a suspect. An investigation had cleared him; yet those types of investigations never blame the cop. "What have you touched, Wendel?"

"Only the phone and the front door coming in." Wendel walked to the door and for the first time saw a helmet on the floor, a biker's helmet like he wore when he took his Yamasaki out on the road. "Oh yes, I also opened the windows and the other doors."

"Are you trying to fuck up the crime scene as much as you fuck up everything else?"

"Pretty obvious the killer came through the front door," Wendel said.

"You shoot this man?"

"He's my friend. I just got home." He pulled out his Paris-LA boarding pass and round-trip itinerary provided by Air France showing how long he had been away.

"You could have come home, killed this man and gone back to France. You own a gun?"

"No, but maybe I should."

"Buy a gun and you'll probably get yourself killed. How do you know this guy?"

Wendel explained he had stayed at Handler's Paris apartment while Handler had enjoyed Wendel's ocean-side home. They had planned to travel California after Wendel's return.

"Are there other ways into the house?" the Chief said. Wendel showed them the walk on the side, where one of the County policemen led them with a strong light to avoid stepping into evidence. The doors in the back opened on either side of the patio, one to the kitchen and the opposite to the bedroom. His heart was beating as though he had just swam a quarter mile in the ocean, and something inside him had dropped to the bottom of his gut. Other than his parents, Handler was his closest friend or relative to die. They met before he married Margo when Handler had just opened his gallery in Paris for up and coming artists. Over the years after Wendel bought a Klee print in

LA that got him interested in art, he bought some paintings that Handler recommended. Their friendship grew enough that his death, his murder, made Wendel feel small and alone.

Off the patio a nearby but fortunately not too nearby skunk had left its calling card. From behind a tree it dashed toward the beach.

"Better keep these doors closed," the Chief said, "especially if someone's out to kill you."

Wendel closed the kitchen door and said, "You going to talk to the neighbors?"

"You think the killer was looking for you?"

"Who else? My friend doesn't know anyone here. It doesn't look like a spoiled a burglary."

The Chief asked one of the detectives to look for signs of a break-in or theft, and then asked Wendel if something had happened that would make someone want to kill him.

"My neighbors have enough money to hire a hit man."

"They don't like you but they've never hurt you or tried to kill you."

Half true, Wendel thought, recalling a day in jail following their complaints, and the day their grandchildren peppered his windows with rocks, probably with encouragement from grandpa.

"Doesn't look like a burglary," said the dispatched detective, "but Mr. Wendel could tell better than me."

So they toured the house. The odor smelled worse which seemed hardly possible. First they checked the living room off the front hall where one of the detectives was taking pictures with a digital camera. Two uniformed policemen with latex gloves used a ballpoint to deposit the helmet into a plastic bag. In the bedroom the king-sized bed was unmade, about how Wendel always left it during the day. Otherwise the master bedroom was intact so that Wendel pictured Handler tippy-toeing in every night so as not to disturb anything he'd then have to clean up. His one suitcase lay in front of the closet, half full, with dirty laundry piled next to it.

"You live alone?" asked the Chief as they looked over the master bath. Wendel said yes and reminded the Chief he was divorced. "Remember the trouble when Margo moved out?" His grown daughter in San Francisco did have a key.

The den looked undisturbed, the paintings and other art objects still there.

"Where's your former wife?" the Chief said.

"She lives in LA, Bel Aire actually," Wendel said, aware how well she had done without him. Not that he had fared badly, and he certainly didn't want her back.

"Ever see her? She ever come down here?"

"No." He thought they'd never get together once Kate was grown, but Margo had called him one day, still the charming voice with the same sense of excitement that had attracted him 25 years earlier, the charm that had landed her in a second marriage to Howard Taylor, the media tycoon whose fashion and publishing subsidiaries Margo now ran. He called her back and they met for coffee about once a year when he was in the city.

"You ride a motorcycle. How about her?"

"Who?"

"Your ex."

"Not while we were together."

"That your helmet?"

He explained that it wasn't, that he guessed his was hanging from its hook in the garage next to his bike. The Chief said he'd take a look later.

"Mind if we take your prints so we can tell which are yours and which aren't?" He didn't object, was surprised how easily the ink washed off in warm water compared to when the army had taken them.

All the furniture was in place in the living room. Pillows were stacked in a corner as though people had been sleeping on the sofas. They were about to walk back to the front hall where the uniformed guys were zipping poor Handler into a bag, when Wendel caught himself. He had thought the art was untouched, but now he saw an empty hook where the Klee print had hung. He pointed this out to the Chief.

"Who's Klee? Is it valuable?"

"A Klee original would be many times more valuable than everything I own put together, but it was a print, like a photo of the original."

"Is this stuff mostly photos?" The Chief waved at the paintings. "What are they worth?"

"Five hundred, maybe a thousand each. The Klee was my only photo, the first thing I ever bought, and I still love it. But it's probably not worth fifty bucks to anyone else. I'll be pissed off if it's gone."

"Better to be pissed off than pissed on," the Chief said. "How big? Could you carry it on a motorcycle?"

"Not very well, probably two feet by three feet, though the frame was simple and not very heavy. It doesn't add up that some biker would want the Klee."

"We'll do the thinking, Wendel," said the Chief.

A wave of energy—anger—rose up through his body over the death of his decent good friend. He could probably do a better job than the Chief thinking through what happened and finding the son-of-a-bitch killer. The Chief was okay, but Wendel was sure he didn't give a damn about Handler, much less the Klee. One thing loving the Klee had taught him was to trust his intuition, just as Klee must have trusted his own to paint such whimsical, child-like figures. His intuition told him the LA Sheriff probably didn't give a damn about this beach-community murder and the Chief could easily write it off as unsolved if he didn't quickly come up with a killer. He hadn't left New York to deal with murder in this one-officer town.

Wendel's anger was carrying him beyond his realm into that of the police, but he couldn't help it. And maybe his abilities and those of the police weren't that far apart. He prided himself as one of the better computer guys around, someone one of the hi-tech behemoths once offered a half million dollars to go to work. Wendel told them he couldn't work for a big company, maybe couldn't work for anyone, so they paid him $100,000 for a one-month gig where Wendel's job was to see how many ways he could break into their systems, so the company could learn how to improve security.

Yes, he could figure this out faster than the police. Thinking through clues was probably no different than studying pages of programming script and data in memory, looking for signs of what had thrown the program into a loop or why data disappeared sometimes but not others. Intuition mattered there, too. Then he realized that back when he was married, Margo would have told him to grow up and leave the murder to the police. "You're immature," she liked to tell him. The marriage counselor agreed, said he'd probably grow up in twenty or thirty years. Maybe sooner. Maybe never.

"This guy, Handler. What more can you tell us about him?"

"Lives in Paris, but he's originally from Germany and Switzerland. The kind of person no one would want to kill, kind, respectful, even gentle. Married, no children, I need to contact his wife."

"Wait a day. We'll call her first. Does she speak English?" He wrote down the contact information.

The rest of the police crew had thinned out and the Chief said they were almost finished for the evening. Then he said, "You got a computer?"

"Sure," Wendel said. "That's how I make a living."

"Can we take a look?"

He led them back to the front porch where he separated his laptop from his suitcase.

"Mind if we take it with us?"

"Yes. I've got a deadline."

"We could get a warrant," the Chief said.

"How long do you need it?"

"A few days."

He said okay. He had backed up onto flash storage before getting onto the plane in Paris, so he'd still have his current projects. He could use his previous laptop that he kept around in case the present one ever crashed, but then he realized the police would probably want it because he had told Handler where to find it if he needed to do email or other business. When the police returned his new laptop, he'd give them the other one.

"Get some fans and rent an ozonator for the house," the Chief said. "After a week you'll hardly know."

Wendel wished it would be that easy.

By the time the crime scene techs, LA detectives and the Chief drove off it was four in the morning, one in the afternoon Paris time. He called Ginette, who should hear about her husband from a sympathetic friend, not a suspicious policeman. First she shrieked and then cried quietly while Wendel listened, at a loss for meaningful words. Before hanging up he said he'd look after the remains and asked if he could help.

Physically exhausted and emotionally spent from Handler's murder, the police, and now the call to Ginette, he thought he might get to sleep. With everyone gone, the smell dominated the house. The yellow pages listed house cleaners that advertised an ozonator and he left a message for when they opened in the morning.

With windows open and the stench a reality, he grabbed a pillow and some blankets and propped himself on a patio lounge chair. Images of Handler flooded his thoughts, followed by a vision of a motorcyclist with a gun at the front door, maybe someone Wendel knew, someone who had come to one of Wendel's Sunday "church services." Perhaps the son-of-a-bitch neighbors hired someone to intimidate or kill him. They had been trying to drive him out of the neighborhood so a buyer could tear down his bungalow and build another mansion. Maybe they hired a cyclist to make it look like it was one of Wendel's guests and then leave the helmet as a misleading clue. But why kill Handler? And was it safe for Wendel to live in the house?

Lying on the lounge chair, he watched an airplane that had departed from LAX ten miles up the coast, turning south and then east after rising above the ocean. The only time he'd taken a red-eye was after he had bought the Klee print on his honeymoon and then talked Margo into returning home to the Midwest in the middle of the night so there might be more room for the picture on the airplane. She never let him forget this sacrifice that she catalogued along with his other shortcomings she kept track of. No one would have killed Handler in order to steal the Klee photo that maybe had appreciated to twenty-five or fifty dollars?

He thought he was dreaming about the killer at the front door when he realized the doorbell was actually ringing. He shot out of the lounge chair with alarm. As quietly as he could he walked around the side of the house, ready to remain in the dark if whoever was there looked like trouble. On the porch stood Henry Gorman along with his Rottweiler, Jugular, Wendel's name, not Gorman's.

2

"What do you want?" Wendal said.

"What are you doing in the bushes?" Gorman said.

"You want to know what I'm doing on my property? What kind of question is that?"

"I saw the police cars. What's going on?"

A good act if Gorman already knew the police were dealing with a homicide. Wendel decided to play it straight, see if he could learn anything, so he related how he had returned and found Handler. "Which raises the question of what are you doing at my front door with your killer dog."

"Sooner or later something like this was bound to happen," Gorman said. "With the types you bring into your house." His agitated voice provoked Jugular who strained at the leash.

"I'm sure you're disappointed it wasn't me," Wendel said, his eyes on the dog.

"Of course not," Gorman said without conviction.

"Like the day I retrieved the kite."

"I was very angry that morning." Gorman's voice was back under control.

One Sunday Wendel had invited his guests to bring their children for a kite-flying contest. When the kids ran their kites up and down the lane, Gorman called the police. The Chief, pissed off over another Sunday call, calmed down all the neighbors except Gorman, who ranted about throwing Wendel in jail, as though he had violated the village's non-existent kite-flying ordinance. Then one of the kites got snagged around an electrical wire, and when Wendel retrieved it, Gorman shouted, "I hope it kills you."

"Anger or not, Chief Pruett knows you're out to get rid of me," Wendel said. "Don't be surprised if you're at the top of his list of suspects."

Jugular showed more impatience, perhaps sensing Gorman's tension. Or maybe it just needed to take a leak.

"I can answer any questions he has."

"Do you collect art?" Wendel said.

"What does that have to do the murder?"

"Whoever killed my friend stole one of my paintings. The Chief will be interested in your collection." Wendel was winging it, grasping for whatever might make Gorman uncomfortable. But Gorman had had enough, and Jugular wanted to move on. Wendel figured that if the dog weren't allowed to rip him apart, it would rather go home than impotently sit at the end of a leash.

Over his shoulder Gorman said, "We won't let you to ruin our neighborhood." As he spoke Jugular lifted a leg and marked Wendel's mailbox as his own.

As Wendel ambled back around the side of the house, he wondered if he was safe in the neighborhood, then decided it didn't matter—he wasn't about to let Gorman and his crowd intimidate him into selling.

Back on the lounge chair he considered the risks. He trusted the Chief even though the taxes on his neighbors' mansions paid a lot more of his salary than Wendel did. Way back the Chief had tipped off Wendel he better pay attention to City Council meetings in which the neighbors were trying to regulate Wendel's 1960s bungalow out of existence or at least Wendel out of the neighborhood. The Chief didn't want ordinances that forced him to monitor how neatly Wendel hung out his laundry or how many decibels his guests' motorcycles generated, or any other ticki-tack law the neighbors tried to pass to encourage Wendel to move and make it less desirable for anyone unlike themselves to live in the village.

The neighbors made the mistake of making churches an exception to their residential-only zoning law. Wendel, the rebel, was an atheist in religious America just as he would have been a devout practitioner in the anti-religion China. He turned his Sunday morning brunches into "church services" with a live rock-gospel band that attracted people of color. An Internet preacher ordained Wendel as a minister in exchange for $25.00. To improve attendance he rented an old school bus and hired a retired driver to bring a load of homeless people eager to feast on the omelets and souffles he liked to cook. When the neighbors tried to amend the law to exclude Wendel's church, the Chief stood up and said the change would violate the First Amendment. This didn't mean the Chief was an ally. He tossed Wendel in jail once when the women took off their tops and merengued with the band down the lane. The Chief had sauntered into Wendel's jail cell with a couple cappuccinos and sat down for a talk. He suggested that Wendel could sell his house for enough money to become as rich as the neighbors.

He must have finally fallen asleep because next he knew something dropped on top of him, shocking him awake.

3

His heart was racing, even in the moment before he realized one of Cheryl Sullivan's cats had jumped onto his lap. He worked the skin on the back of Leo's neck (or was it Luella?) as he watched the dawn work its way through the coastal fog. The sense that someone was watching him made him squint even though he could hardly distinguish a straight-back chair ten feet in front of himself. He ratcheted the lounge chair up a couple notches and then heard, "Wendel. You're awake."

The words startled him until he recognized Cheryl's voice. "Getting there," he said as she sat down on the chair. "How long have you been here," he said as he rubbed his eyes. Already he was alert and full of energy, in part because it was the middle of the afternoon in Paris.

"What happened to Handler?" Cheryl said. "You were hosting the entire police force last night, and then one of them came over, told me he was dead and asked me all kinds of questions."

"I found him when I walked into the house. Someone murdered him."

"That's terrible. I looked in on him while you were away like you asked. Seemed like a nice guy. He even used the hot tub a few times. I think he's gay."

"He went both ways," Wendel said as he added gay-tryst-gone-bad to his mental list of reasons for Handler's murder. He scooted to the edge of the lounge chair where he did some stretches and from where Cheryl came into better focus, wrapped in her bathrobe made out of the sable coat her mother had bequeathed her. She was the one neighbor Wendel liked, dating back twenty years to when he and Margo and Cheryl and Greg unsuccessfully tried to grow into their marriages. Greg used to join Wendel for beers after work and complain about how Cheryl spent two dollars for every one he earned. Meanwhile Cheryl and Margo got together on weekends and complained about their husbands' lack of imagination with foreplay. After Margo split, Cheryl and Greg both complained to Wendel about the other, making him realize that a marriage counselor was nothing more than a listener.

He especially appreciated Cheryl. Even though he knew he could never get along with the rich, arrogant, self-centered, self-entitled sons-of-bitches who owned the property around him and thought they owned the world, he still missed a sense of neighborhood. When he was growing up, the kids all played together. The parents were modest, even the rich and talented. One of his fondest memories was Tommy Glass's mother—she could have bought 10 sable coats—hiding him in her clothes hamper so she could wheel him down the street to the big sycamore in his yard that was home base for hide-and-seek. Wendel hopped out of the hamper and freed all the people Tommy had captured.

"Do you know anything that helped the police?" he asked.

"Not really. They were interested in some bikers who came by one day while you were away, but I don't think they stayed long. I think Handler asked them in, but the place probably didn't seem the same without you."

He thought for a moment—maybe one of them left the helmet, though not very likely.

"Someone stole one of my paintings, a Paul Klee. Actually an inexpensive print. Did Handler mention the Klee?"

"He was fascinated by it. For half an hour in the hot tub one night he told me all about Klee. He was from the Baja, I think."

Wendel smiled as he imagined Cheryl not listening very closely to Handler's description of the Bauhaus school of art. She was probably busy probing with her toes only to learn he was gay. Ironic, Wendel thought, that Cheryl, who had no interest in Bauhaus art, embodied much of Bauhaus's whimsy. He started to explain, but Cheryl interrupted.

"Whatever. I need a bottle from the wine cellar for tonight. Okay to get it."

Even though Cheryl had a key, she always asked when he was around. He got up and together they walked out to the backyard to retrieve one of the valuable bottles she got in her divorce settlement.

The wine cellar was actually one of those bomb shelters built in the 50s and 60s in response to Russia's thirst for larger nukes than America had. The underground temperatures and built-in ventilation were perfect for Cheryl's collection, though hardly necessary for Wendel's ten-dollar chardonnays and pinot noirs.

He climbed down an unstable metal ladder that seemed out of place in space that was plusher than Wendel's house—leather easy chairs, upholstered sofa, high-end bunk beds, granite kitchen counters that weren't so common back then. When he helped Cheryl off the ladder, her robe fell open. "Oops," she said as she pulled it together around her well-maintained body and ample breasts. Wendel fantasized dropping out of life to retire to the shelter that was built for uninterrupted occupancy for at least a year. He'd have his computer, lots of books and plenty of food, and whenever Cheryl came for a bottle of wine, they'd make passionate love.

"Grab what you want," he said. As Cheryl studied her collection, he noticed that the one book he kept next to the easy chair was gone. "Did you come down while I was away?"

"I got a bottle and showed Handler the shelter. He said he lived in East Germany when the U.S. and Russia were making more and more nukes. His family got out before the wall went up."

"I don't see my copy of *On the Beach*."

"He might have borrowed it."

"Looks like you're planning a special dinner," he said pointing at the bottle she had chosen.

"Just some guy who played for the Raiders until he blew out his knee. Claims he spent a lot of time in Napa, that they have the best wines."

"You're going to educate him?"

Wendel sometimes kicked himself that he had fallen into a platonic friendship with Cheryl, each of them connecting with the other over their formerly married status. He felt privileged to hear about her romantic forays. Her long-term relationships lasted about two weeks. When they both relaxed, naked, in her hot tub, she'd give him more details than he needed, yet he couldn't bring himself to cut her off. He'd love to audition, but was afraid he'd get two weeks of sex and lose a satisfying friendship.

After they climbed up the ladder and replaced the lock, she said, I read that women peak sexually in their forties, while men start to fade at eighteen. I thought I'd grab this linebacker before he falls apart."

"Young studs are great when you want five or six quickies," he said. "Someday you'll find a guy as old as that '59 Chateau La Mission Haut Brion you're about to waste on the stud. We need a few years like a fine bottle of wine."

"Do you have someone in mind?"

"Not at the moment," he said as he let go of her hand he had taken to help her out of the shelter. But the right time might come, he thought. He dated several women he enjoyed and who didn't want to become emotionally involved.

At the break in the hedge between their yards, they kissed, her lips slightly parted. She always kissed him that way, even when she was married to Greg, and her kiss always left him wanting more. One of these days, he thought as he walked back to his house.

Upstairs in his office, he couldn't tell whether Handler had used his old Dell laptop. If so he had put it back on the shelf, front-to-rear beneath his printer, just as Wendel had left it. A breeze made the odor more bearable as it blew through the second floor windows facing the ocean and then out the front where Wendel sat at his desk. He powered up the Dell and returned to the kitchen to start the coffee, making a note to pick up an espresso maker next time he drove to LA. A modern one like Handler's apartment had in Paris that maybe Margo could help him buy at the Design Center.

Back at the computer he inserted a program he had written to search memory and drives while leaving no tracks. Data flashed onto the screen in binary form, 1's and 0's. F5 converted the binary to English. The Chief would have fucked this up for sure. Even the FBI sometimes asked for his help. Next he accessed the control panel and changed the date to two days hence. He figured he could change it back before turning it over to the police in a couple days, so that if he discovered anything important, they would think that he had turned it over as soon as he discovered it. Remembering details was never his strength so he made a note to change back the date.

He opened his own email program and was in luck. Handler had used Wendel's email rather than access his own server. It was 8:35, time to re-call the house cleaners about the ozonator. "A living room, dining room, three bedrooms, den, kitchen and the large room upstairs, about 2,500 square feet," he responded to their questions, and they said they'd be down from Venice in an hour or so.

Back at the computer he thanked Miss Gilbert for kicking his butt in tenth grade French and went to work. For Handler's first week, all the emails were about business: the gallery's request to lower its price on a Magnolo by 200 Euros beneath Magnolo's authorized price, Handler's email to Magnolo asking permission, Magnolo's email back wanting half of the 200 to come out of Handler's commission, Handler's gracious response that he'd absorb the entire 200 but had wanted to ask anyway, etc. etc.

From about a week ago, the day Wendel had taken a train to Beaune for a Burgundy festival, an email popped up that startled him. "Jacob, Attached is a photo of what appears to be a Klee print. I've never seen this Klee and wonder if you have and if you know who owns the original." Wendel switched to the file of deleted emails to find the answer, but before he could locate it, a Jeep Wendel didn't recognize pulled into his driveway. Nor did he recognize either the man or woman who got out.

"Can I help you," he called out the window.

They answered that they were from the Times, making him wish for a moment, but only a moment, he had allowed the neighbors to install a gate and watchmen on the lane. He called down that he was tied up right now. The man replied that he sailed a 27' sloop, was a knot expert, and offered to come upstairs and untie him. Amused, Wendel gave in, walked down and opened the door.

"You should get your information from the police," he said in answer to a question about the murder.

"They told us this man Handler was your house sitter."

"Yes."

"How do you know him? The police say he's from Paris and is survived by his wife."

The Times suburban writers gave sympathetic coverage to Wendel's village-council disputes with his neighbors, so Wendel didn't want to appear uncooperative, even though these two were not the usual reporters. He explained that he and Handler had been friends for years and answered a few other questions, and it soon became clear they knew about as much as he, not counting the emails he wanted to get back to. "I'm still in shock," he said, "and with jet lag. Why don't you come back in a few days and I'll answer anything I know."

They parried several other questions until a patrol car drove into the driveway. Damn, Wendel thought. His shoulders clenched as he realized he should have hidden the laptop before coming downstairs.

The Chief climbed out of the sedan and ambled up the walk. "What've you told them you didn't tell me?" he said.

"Not a thing, of course," Wendel said.

"Excuse us," the Chief said to the reporters. "We'll let you know if there's something new."

Inside Wendel offered to share the coffee, which the Chief declined. "If my French is any good," he said, "Handler's wife said you called. After I told you not to."

"I thought she deserved to hear from a friend rather than the police."

"Look Wendel. The murder is not your usual neighborhood dispute. I'm running the show. I don't care if you flew here last night. You're still a suspect and better not interfere with my investigation."

Wendel fought back a comment about washed up big city cops still wanting to play police and said, "I understand."

"I doubt that you do, Wendel. The wife thinks her husband was here on business. That true?"

"News to me. Makes me wonder if he did something with the missing Klee."

"Missing what?"

"The Paul Klee painting."

"Tell us everything you know about Handler," the Chief said as he plopped himself onto a barstool at the counter between the den and the kitchen.

Wendel realized he didn't know that much. He described Handler's modest apartment he shared with Ginette, with whom he no longer shared a bed. He explained how the gallery specialized in little-known artists. He was pretty sure Handler was bi-sexual, which possibly had something to do with the murder. The Chief seemed interested and made a note before saying, "I'll have to add your prejudice about sexual preference to your other faults, Wendel. Was Handler here the entire week?"

Before Wendel could answer, the doorbell rang and the Chief indicated that he should answer. The house cleaners had arrived, and Wendel escorted them through the bungalow as they identified where to put fans and ozonators. When they reached the den, the Chief wasn't there. Wendel looked outside and stepped out on the patio to check the yard. When he returned, he heard, "Wendel, get up here now."

Dammit. He found the computer. Wendel climbed the stairs and was immediately relieved that his screen-saver program had replaced the email list with a dark screen.

"What the hell is this?"

"An old computer I no longer use."

"That's why it's sitting out because you no longer use it."

I have work to do and you took mine."

"Maybe Handler did some business on it."

"We could find out," Wendel said moving toward the console, hoping to delete the email file without the Chief seeing.

"Don't touch it," the Chief said. "I'm taking it in."

"Hey, return my other one first."

"Sorry."

"Then get a warrant," Wendel said, arms crossed over his chest, unable to hide his anger. "You can't just come in here and take away my livelihood. Besides"—he struggled to regain his composure—"if Handler used my email, you'll probably destroy the evidence." Wendel believed this was true unless a professional did the work. Then he realized he had been careless. He should have dumped both the memory and the hard drive onto an external hard drive so he'd have backup.

"I'm taking it right now," the Chief said. "No warrant. Sue me. By the time you win, you'll have it back. That is unless you have something to hide. You should have turned this over last night."

Wendel had no hope of stopping the Chief. As he cooled off, he realized he could buy a new computer for a few hundred bucks and get right back to where he was.

"Go ahead and take it," he said. "But let me unplug it so you don't fuck up the rest of my equipment." The Chief stepped aside so that Wendel was able to cut the power before the Chief saw the open email file. Wendel held his breath that the battery was too worn down to take over, which turned out to be true.

As he walked the Chief to the car after answering a few more questions, he said, "If I buy a new computer to make some money, are you going to take it too?"

"You better have a receipt with a date and a serial number I can check."

4

Needing a computer, Wendel checked the phone book for the nearest Circuit City or Best Buy with minimal traffic between him and them. Nothing looked good, so he grabbed the flash storage from his vacation and drove to GeTechNome, an Orange County biotech client whom he was assisting on a major project. GeTechNome was establishing telecommuting systems that allowed employees to work at home if a pandemic or terrorist attack prevented them from going to the office. Once established, the systems would be used at least once a week for practice and as a contribution to the nation's effort to save gasoline. Wendel's role was to develop the security system that would prevent hackers from stealing secrets.

When he turned south onto Highland Avenue he noticed a uniformed man at his corner. It didn't look like a police uniform and when he tried to get a better look in the rear view mirror, he saw an unusual-looking Chevy turn after him from the lane to the east of Highland. The Chevy—an old Corvair he was pretty sure—followed him onto Highway 1, exited when he got off in Newport Beach, but drove on past when he stopped to pick up some bagels, cream cheese and lox. Back on the road he wondered if the Chief was keeping track of him. If so Handler's death was becoming a cheap detective novel.

"Welcome back, Wendel," said Margie, the receptionist in the IT corner of the first floor. "We've missed the bagels and schmear."

"How about me?" he said.

"We miss you too. Just don't show up without the goodies."

"The way to your heart is through your taut little tummy," he said.

"Sexual harassment," she called out. Margie, who emanated perfume, a hint of orange and rose, had already been involved in two sexual harassment claims involving men in the department, both claims having been made by the men. She kept the sign-in sheet in her desk so that when her favorites fetched it to sign in, she called out in a loud voice to keep their hands out of her drawers.

"I take it back," he said. "There is no way to your heart. You're heartless."

"Speaking of heartless," she said, "Sally Simms left a message for you to drop by and see her next time you came in."

"Careful what you say about Sally. She's my favorite. After you. You got a free conference room or office plus a computer I can use?"

Stevens, the department head, found him both, switched on the spare desktop and was about to walk out when Wendel asked, "Any idea why Simms wants to see me?"

"Some of the scientists don't like the project, the idea of working at home. They're afraid of security. Whatever they want, Simms gets for them," Stevens said. "They run this company."

Simms, GeTechNome's research coordinator, once told Wendel that the IT geeks lost sight that scientific research made their jobs possible. The computer people resented how effectively she looked after the scientists, even pampered them.

"They're not dropping the project, I hope." Wendel said. His work was nearly complete and he pictured his results and most of his fee in the trash.

"Simms supports it, but she has to keep the children happy."

When Stevens left him alone, Wendel tried to reenter his email account but found it blocked by the server. That was quicker than he gave the Chief credit for. He didn't have with him his utility program that would allow him to bypass the block, so he tried to remember the name of the person Handler had emailed, pretty sure it was Berger or Burgher. He googled both names along with Klee and shortly came up with something called Der Klee Entwurf in Lucerne Switzerland.

Without much difficulty he entered the Entwurf's email system, searched for "Photo of Klee Print," and found Jacob Burgher's reply to Handler's message. "Your Klee print is *'falschung.'*" Wendel had a pretty good idea what the word meant but pulled down a German-English dictionary to confirm. A "fake" or "phony." The email continued that Klee never painted this picture. "The signature, what we call *'der sendezeichen,'* is too large for Klee, plus there are more subtle clues about *'der schwindel.'* Keep in touch, Jacob." Wow, Wendel thought. He never believed the print was worth anything but had assumed it was at least a copy of a real Klee. Occasionally in museum bookstores he had thumbed through heavy, portfolio-sized books of Klee art and had never found a reference to the original. Now he knew why. Actually his three-dollar investment was more interesting to him as a fraud than as a cheap copy of an original. Plus the painting posed a new mystery—why would anyone steal a copy of a fake? A wild guess said that the answer would lead to Handler's murderer.

Guards on the second floor, the research center, verified Wendel's security status. GeTechNome had required elaborate security checks when Wendel became involved, and he guessed that some of the research had national security implications. While he waited for Sally Simms inside the metal detector, he gazed out the reception area window. To his dismay he spied the Corvair. First a chill ran down his spine and then his chest contracted. It had to be the same—how many those "unsafe-at-any-speed" dinosaurs were around? Was someone waiting for him down there or was someone from GeTechNome following him?

Sally Simms greeted him with a warm smile and a California hug that others had warned him not to trust. He had never had a problem with her, but then again he always accepted whatever persona people showed, and if later they wanted conflict or even a fight, he could enjoy that as well. Except in a romance. The Margo experience had left him wary of any committed relationship. He considered asking Simms who owned the Corvair, but she was already walking toward the labs.

"I want to meet with Waldo Peterson, our Nobel Laureate," she said and took his arm and guided him down the corridor. "Waldo has doubts about working at home and is raising security issues." From when Wendel had interviewed all the scientists to gain input for the project, he recalled that Peterson had been unavailable or unwilling to meet. Wendel had learned that Peterson had discovered something beyond esoteric, something Wendel couldn't understand when he read about it in a GeTech-Nome brochure, something that presumably made the world a better place, the kind of feat Wendel admired and sometimes unrealistically imagined he would someday accomplish.

Simms led him into a spacious office-laboratory flaunting an unpleasant chemical odor, though he had smelled worse in his high school lab. With stacks of papers on the floor all around him, Peterson lay back in a recliner with a wireless keyboard in his lap. He looked asleep, but when Simms put her hand on his shoulder, he glanced up. After Simms explained why they were meeting, Wendel said, "I'm always looking for a better environment for creative work. Would you mind telling me about yours?"

"I remember you, the computer genius," Peterson said. "I need to teach you the facts of life in the research world." He climbed out of the recliner and looked directly at Wendel, about two feet from his nose, his recently-minted breath in Wendel's face. On the wall behind him was a large picture of Peterson in a tux accepting his Nobel Prize. "I'm not putting control of my work on a computer so that some smart young guy like you has access to it."

Wendel started to answer, but Peterson interrupted him. "I don't care what security you put in. I'm not using it."

"What if we have a pandemic or terrorist attack that keeps us all away?" Simms said.

"I'd still come in."

"Authorities might not let you."

"If I can't outfox Homeland Security, I don't deserve to come in."

"My kind of guy," Wendel said. "We'll come in together so you can invent the cure for bird flu and then try it out on me."

Peterson stared at Wendel for a moment and then said, "I'm not your kind of guy because I don't secretly steal things like you online hacks do." Peterson's vehemence pushed Wendel back a step. The possibility flashed through his mind that the scientist might take a swing at him. Peterson was at least ten years older but he looked like he spent time at the gym and could do some harm. Wendel's shock from last night was obviously fueling his paranoia, and he needed to regain his composure.

"Waldo, none of our scientists will be required to use this system," Simms said. "Still it wouldn't hurt for Wendel to explain the security measures he plans to install. You're so curious about everything in the world."

Wendel took a deep breath, appreciative of Simms' tact. Peterson gave a curt okay and Wendel started in. He generally described a system of codes and passwords they would keep in a vault, multiple firewalls, and electronic sentries that would track every entry into the system and hunt down and identify intruders. He still had to research codes and promised to make a full security presentation to Peterson and all the scientists, "for your information even if you don't want to use it."

Simms and Wendel walked back to her modest office, not a quarter the size of Peterson's. She explained that Peterson came from a cutthroat academic background where scientists fabricate research results to get tenure and grants. Many try to take advantage of what others are doing so they can be the first to publish.

"I think I can satisfy them," Wendel said with more optimism than he felt.

"If not?"

"The program is voluntary. Some will do it and others will follow when they see it works."

Frances Holmes, who had founded and still ran GeTechNome, had originally rejected a proposal to put research on line. She thought the security challenges were too great and was concerned that someone had already stolen some of their secrets. An expert at Science Research Associates located at Stanford University had recommended Wendel, who convinced her to give it a try. Wendel told her he was excited by the challenge and willing to work for nothing until the installation was complete when Frances could pay him what she thought his work was worth. He pictured losing the entire GeTechNome fee and falling behind on his payments to the IRS for taxes he still didn't understand why he owed. He had taken some stock in a dot-com company as a fee and even though the stock sank to nothing after first soaring, he owed this monstrous tax. Every year his accountant prepared his tax return and told him he was house-poor and short of cash. "You won't be able to borrow forever against your home to pay your bills," she said. She likened his money management to a Ponzi scheme. "Your house is worth a lot because it's next to the ocean, but one of these days it'll fall down because you can't afford to patch the rot and paint it."

"What I need to do," he said to Simms as he leaned forward and unblinkingly engaged her eyes, "is to come up with a system I can't secretly break into."

"Meet that challenge or this project's dead," she said. "I'm a big supporter of what you're doing, but that's the reality."

He told her he'd present his solution in a week. If they were satisfied, they could implement the system and run some test experiments, let the scientists experience some hands-on work.

He was so focused on satisfying the scientists that he again forgot to ask Simms about the Corvair as she walked him to the stairs. The car was still in the parking lot, no driver in sight. Maybe one of the scientists was so opposed to the new system that he tried to kill Wendel and found Handler instead. He fought off the idea as utter paranoia, yet still he checked the rearview mirror every minute or so as he drove home. At the entrance to his lane, a Humbie stretched across the road so he couldn't get past. Next to it stood the uniformed man he had seen earlier or a look-alike in a similar uniform.

5

"Can I help you, bud?" The guard looked down at Wendel and his twelve-year old Honda with the kind of disdain he'd show the pizza delivery boy.

"Yeah, get your armor out of my way."

"What's your business?"

"None of yours," Wendel said.

"Look Bud, this is a private street."

"Who says?"

"The owners."

"I'm one of the owners. Get that thing out of here."

The guard pulled a piece of paper from his pocket and said," What's your name, sir?"

"Either move or I'm calling the police." Wendel fished his phone from the cup holder.

"Please tell me your name?" The guard's voice had lost its certainty.

Wendel punched his auto-dial number for time and temperature and after a moment said, "May I speak to Chief Pruett. This is Wendel."

"Mr. Wendel. Please, Mr. Gorman would like to see you," the guard said in a voice obviously miffed that he had to kowtow to Wendel. "Follow me."

He turned the ugly yellow Humbie that blew out a fog of exhaust and drove up the lane. Wendel followed to his own driveway where he turned in. The guard swung around and stopped at the end of the drive where Wendel told him he'd call the police back if the man came onto his property. "Tell Mr. Gorman I'm busy. I'm busy all day."

Inside he climbed the stairs to check on-line for his most recent bank statement to see how much his loan payments were, how bad off he'd be if he lost the GeTech-Nome fee. He stopped short when he realized he had no computer. Nor did he receive bank statements by mail because he valued doing business on line and didn't want to waste the paper. Maybe they'd give him the information over the phone, but when he called, the robot kept him on hold for ten minutes of mom and apple pie music, interrupted every minute by an automated announcement that someone would be with him shortly. He ought to hack into the bank's music system and substitute some decent jazz. Instead he slammed down the phone, and immediately it rang.

"Yes."

"Your usual pleasant voice, sweetheart," Margo said.

"Sorry. The bank had me on hold forever."

"I can recommend some medicine for your emotions," she said.

"Sure," he said, falling back on the old the habit of not contradicting Margo. And why should he? Her medicine apparently worked well on her emotions. Occasionally he took half a low-dose Valium for insomnia, but he prided himself on not needing the pills she took to function.

"Try some Ativan," she said. "I may have some business for you. Howard's looking for someone to evaluate his companies' I.T. needs, someone who's independent who's not selling anything. I told him about you."

"Tell me how much I'm paying a month on a million-four loan at six and three-fourths, and I'll tell you whether I need the business," he said as he looked for a pencil to write down the answer.

"You're not very grateful," she said. "Look at your loan papers.... Okay, I get it. You're no more business-like than when we were married. And broke. How many years is your loan?"

"I think thirty."

"Checking Google...Why don't you check Google... Here it is. A million-four...How about nine thousand and change a month," she said.

"I'm interested," he said, and she told him she'd tell her husband. Wendel had read that the guy was a son-of-a-bitch. If he couldn't get Taylor's consulting job and ran low on money, he could sell his house to him on condition that he continue to give the neighbors a fit.

"You sound like something's bothering you more than usual," she said.

He raised his feet onto the open bottom desk drawer and told her about Handler and dealing with the police half the night. She responded with silence. After a moment he said, "You still there?"

"I'm stunned."

"You remember him?" Back when they met Handler in Paris, Margo had liked him, even flirted with him, which had pissed Wendel off.

"Kind of," she said, though without Margo's usual certainty, as though she remembered him more than she wanted to let on. She wasn't the type to care after all these years.

"Whoever killed him took that Klee painting you hated. At least I know it wasn't you."

She told him she was sorry and that she had to run. Again the phone rang as soon as he put it down.

"Hi Sweetheart." It was Cheryl.

"Nice to hear your voice," he said. And nice to be called sweetheart, he thought.

"Guess who called," she said.

"What's he want?" When Gorman wanted to talk with Wendel, he used Cheryl as the go-between.

"Because of your friend's murder, he wants to gate the lane." The homeowner's association that Wendel refused to join couldn't erect a gate because it was a public street. They could ask the city to abandon the street only if all the property owners petitioned, so Wendel had a veto.

"I hate gated communities. The answer's no."

"I hate them too, but I'm scared."

"The murder was either a random thing or meant for me," Wendel said. "You don't have anything to worry about."

"Will you do me a favor and talk with him."

The power move would be to make Gorman come to him, but he didn't want the guy in his home. He was about to agree to walk down to Gorman's place when he thought about the odor. "Tell him to come on down," he said. "Without the dog. You come too, to keep him calm."

Gorman walked up the drive dressed in Bermuda shorts that modeled his spindly legs and a yellow sports shirt with an emblem Wendel didn't recognize, probably for some snooty club. About all he knew about the man was that he had sold his company a while back for a lot of money. Wendel assumed his employees hated him and were relieved to see him go. Now Gorman didn't have enough to do so he tried to organize the neighborhood. At least he doesn't hide his baldhead, Wendel thought as he opened the door.

"Henry, come on in. You look more relaxed than last night. Cheryl's coming, so have a seat." Gorman sniffed but didn't say anything about the smell, which was even more pungent despite the fans and ozonator. Santa Ana winds, not unusual for the middle of September, brought ninety-degree temperatures oozing the odor out of the walls.

"Sure you wouldn't like to come down to my place for wine and steak tartar?"

"Thanks but I have lots of work to do so we need to make this quick. I have some Charles Shaw Chardonnay if you want a glass."

Gorman declined—Wendel didn't have to admit he had no Charles Shaw—and sank into the soft easy chair he had inherited from his mother. "Shall we turn that off for a few minutes," Gorman said, gesturing toward the noisy fan across the room.

"The house cleaners said I need to keep them on," Wendel said. He got up to greet Cheryl who was walking up the drive. She apparently didn't want Gorman to observe her coming through the hedge and letting herself in off the patio—too much intimacy with the enemy.

After they were seated, Gorman said, "We need to reach an agreement to protect ourselves in this neighborhood."

"And...," Wendel said. In addition to having offered in the past to buy Wendel's property, Gorman had offered to pay for Wendel to tear down the bungalow and build a modern house. He had offered up to $600 a foot for up to 3000 square feet. In exchange for that million-eight Wendel would have to join the neighborhood association and agree to the bylaws. Wendel was curious to see how Gorman would outdo that offer.

"What can we do?" Gorman said. "You tell us."

"One theory I have is that you're making a big deal about the gate and the guard with his armor in order to cover up that it's you who wants me dead. That you hired a killer who found my unfortunate friend instead of me the other night."

"Ridiculous," Gorman said.

"You didn't tell me last night whether you collect art?"

"I do."

"Modern art?"

"So what?"

"Because it makes you a stronger suspect."

"You're crazy," Gorman said.

"That's a strong reaction," Wendel said. He had provoked Gorman to throw him off guard, but had probably gone too far to incite the man to reveal meaningful information. If he had meaningful information. "If I'm crazy, why not humor me rather than tell me I'm crazy?"

"You're paranoid."

"Henry," Cheryl said. "When you find a dead friend in your house you become a little paranoid."

"You're right. I'm sorry about your friend," Gorman said. "I should have said so." He sank back into his chair as though someone had pulled the plug and let out the air. Wendel had never seen Gorman absent his CEO veneer that survived even in short pants. If he had a contract out for Wendel, he at least had the decency to regret the collateral damage.

"I can't think of anything I need," Wendel said.

"If you don't want a new house, how about some cash. Give it to charity if you don't like money."

"How about a million-four to pay off my mortgage."

"That's a little steep," Gorman said.

"You offered a million-eight before."

"To upgrade your house. No more 1950s bungalow."

"Forget it. I don't want the money anyway."

"Think about it, Wendel," Cheryl said. You don't have to decide now." She used that voice woman were so good at when they wanted to puff up a man to preserve his ego while getting him to agree with her. "You're so creative. There's probably something you do want."

"It is stuffy in here," Wendel said. "Let's sit on the patio."

Wendel opened a decent white Burgundy, while considering how much he could get from Gorman by agreeing to the guard and nothing more. Just in case he lost the GeTechNome fee. He carried out the wine, some glasses, and some of Handler's cheese he had never seen before, Sainte Nectaire. After he sat down, he said, "A man in a Corvair followed me this morning. Was that one of your guys, Henry?"

"No," Gorman said. "We hired only the guards."

"Are you sure? Do you need to ask your guy out front? I thought that if you're not trying to kill me, that you might be trying to scare me."

"Maybe we all ought to be scared," Gorman said as he found his phone and presumably called the guard service. After signing off he confirmed that the driver of the Corvair wasn't part of his program.

"I'll think about it," Wendel said. "In the meantime you can keep your guard out there. By the way I spent the morning at my lawyer's office, changing my will. If I die by other than natural causes, this property will belong forever to a gospel-loving church, hopefully to operate an amusement park for kids."

Cheryl laughed and signaled Gorman to keep quiet. She said Wendel's estate plan was fine, they'd all say prayers for him, but it didn't matter because nothing was going to happen to him. His daughter and grandchildren would end up with the house, hopefully they would be less ornery but just as much fun. "Henry, the grandkids hate gospel music," she said.

They finished the wine, struggling to talk about the Dodgers—Cheryl rolled her eyes—and then beach erosion.

When they left, Wendel walked as far Cheryl's house where the two of them chatted and Wendel declined her offer to meet the linebacker who was due any time. He envied the linebacker and not just for the passionate evening ahead. For the first time in years he wished he didn't live alone.

Back at the house, the light was blinking on his answering machine. He brought in the wine, glasses and cheese and while cleaning up played the message. "Mr. Handler, this is Victor Zvolens in Salinas. Sorry I didn't answer sooner but I was away for a few days. Yes, I do own several Paul Klee paintings. I have something to tell you about the print you described. Call my private extension, 831-424-5544." Wendel perked up. Handler had more than a passing interest in the Klee painting, and Wendel couldn't help believing the painting was connected to his death. He wondered when Handler called Zvolens. Must have been before he found out from Burgher the painting was a fake.

He dialed but the private number routed him to a recording that said it was after five—he had lost track of time—and that the vineyard would be open in the morning. He could probably figure out what vineyard and then break into their computer system, maybe learn something about Zvolens, which reminded him he needed to get one of his laptops back or buy a new one. Suddenly he realized how quickly his ethics had slid or maybe crashed was a better word. In college he had vowed never to break into a computer system illegally. In any event before talking with Zvolens, he needed to figure out what he'd ask him.

6

Exhausted, he sank onto a lounge chair, aware of how stressful the day had been—finding Handler dead, losing both computers, threat of losing the GeTechNome project, his flagging finances. He even considered accommodating Gorman's gate, which made him wonder if he was getting old, running out of energy? Maybe he fit a study that said hardened criminals become pussycats after a certain age. Wendel was pretty sure he was younger than that age. Besides he valued being a rebel and didn't want to give it up.

The cold awakened him about 10, the wind having moved around to the northwest off the ocean. Hungry, he slid into his shoes and headed to In 'n Out Burger. The guard at the head of the lane waved him through, apparently alerted that the guy in the old Honda who looked like a beach bum was okay. At the drive-through Wendel bought the poor guy a couple of burgers.

On the way home he handed the guard the bag and thinking he must be bored to death and in need of something to do, Wendel asked, "What do you think about the murder? Did the victim walk in on a burglary or was someone out to kill him?"

"Burglars don't kill people. Maybe downtown LA. Not out here."

"Did they tell you it was in my house?"

"No offense, but no burglar would bother with your house. I'm sure the others are all wired, so he'd stay out of this neighborhood."

"Maybe the murder's a she and not a he," Wendel said.

"Buddy, thanks for the burgers, but I don't need someone besides my wife complaining that I always say 'he.'"

Back on the lounge chair, Wendel scooped the smothered onions off the buns with his front teeth a few at a time before getting into to the cheeseburgers. He couldn't get the guard's opinions out of his mind. The killer had probably come for Handler or himself, maybe for the Klee print, which wasn't a random burglary. Years before when he had told Handler about the print, Handler had told him that Klee painted from his unconscious mind, which evoked visual images. Handler explained that images came from the right side of the brain. Wendel's images came in words and ideas from the left side of the brain. Something told him that visual imaging like Klee had mastered would help solve the murder, but Wendel wasn't any good at visual images. Soon his thoughts put him to sleep.

Shock catapulted him out of the chair when he felt a hand, a cold hand, on his shoulder.

"Easy, my friend," said a familiar voice. "It's Brendan."

"What in the hell are you doing here?" Wendel said as he tried to clear his eyes. When he did, the sight of Brendan Wilde's naked body dripping water, greeted him.

"You got a pair of shorts I can borrow?" Brendan said.

"If I do, they'll be too big around your macho waist. What are you doing?"

"When I drove up on my bike, the big dude at the lane wouldn't let me in. I tried to call you, but I guess you didn't hear it inside and your cell's off. So I drove up to the public beach and swam down."

"Has to be a mile," Wendel said.

"Good exercise."

Wendel could never figure Brendan out. They met at a motorcycle rally several years back and had been friends ever since. After parachuting into Grenada in 1979, he had resigned from the Navy Seals because he didn't want to fight the cold war against helpless islanders. Wendel imagined that Navy Seals were gung-ho choir boys who sincerely pledged allegiance to the flag and one nation under God but still had enough pent-up aggression to kill people with their bare hands. Brendan meanwhile was a gentle atheist. His goal in life was to find adventure, all the better if the adventure were dangerous, and best of all if the adventure risked his life. Wendel enjoyed biking with him and only wished he could acquire a modest part of his friend's talent for not working.

"Get the shorts and a safety pin, and give me a lift back to the public beach so we can get some breakfast."

"I don't have a helmet for you."

"That's why I'm here. I dropped by a few weeks ago with my survivalist buddies and met your friend. Nice guy. I drove off without my helmet to get some food, but never got back because I got a call my mother had fallen down. Had to scoot down to San Diego."

"You have a problem, my friend," Wendel said.

"You gave away my helmet?"

Wendel described his return from Paris, finding Handler along with the helmet in the front hall, how the police wearing plastic gloves and using a ballpoint pen dropped the helmet into an evidence bag. He watched Brendan react, aware for the first time, though probably unconsciously aware from the beginning, how inscrutable the man was. Did Brendan show dismay or was it Wendel's imagination when he said Handler had been shot.

"On your feet," Brendan said. "Get me down to the beach. I want to go by the police station and plead my case."

"Why the hell do you hang around with survivalists? They're right-wing radicals."

"They like to rock-climb and live off the land. Not a lot of people in that league."

Wendel's head had cleared and he started to grasp that the Nazis or survivalists or whatever they were called had been in the house. He also felt a little ridiculous questioning the naked Brendan Wilde, but he couldn't let go.

"What are survivalists doing down here? I thought they lived in the woods in Idaho or grew dope in northern California."

"We did a week of desert training in the Mohave. A lot different than up north. Let's get going. This is a good way to catch hypothermia "

As he stood up, Wendel said, "You left those guys here with Handler when you went down to San Diego?"

"I phoned them when I couldn't come back and I think they left, but you're right, it does create a question."

After tossing Brendan a swimsuit and sweatshirt, Wendel put some coffee on to drip and went to brush his teeth and take a shower. He needed to call Victor what's-his-name in Salinas but that might take some time. Better to wait until he got home and Brendan was off somewhere else. In the shower he thought about how finding Handler's killer was becoming an obsession. What would he do if he found him? It wasn't as though he knew how to use a gun or was equipped for hand-to-hand combat in a fight with one of these guys who knew how to survive in the woods and the desert. His last fight was over who got to use the swing in kindergarten.

The guard, one Wendel hadn't seen, was taken by surprise by two men on a motorcycle. Maybe he recognized Brendan as the guy he had turned away. "It's Wendel," he said as he pulled to a stop and took off his helmet. It was a different man from the one he had bought the burgers for. "I'm the guy you're supposed to humor."

"Good morning, Mr. Wendel. Sorry to stop you."

"I have biker friends you need to let in. Check it out with Gorman. We need a way to let them through."

"Yes sir," the guard said provoking Wendel to give Brendan a gentle elbow to the ribs to underscore the uncharacteristic respect shown him by a man in uniform.

"By the way. I thought you might be able to use some fresh coffee." Wendel handed the guard a thermos he had poured some into.

The police station, an old downtown store probably built around the same time as Wendel's house, sat on a street with wall-to-wall stores, mostly chains, and stood out as the only structure that looked like it was built before last week. The jail had a couple cells for people who needed to sleep it off, but Wendel was pretty sure they shipped felons, if they ever caught one, to LA County. The police station also had Myrna, the Chief's latest part-time office help, all from the same sorority at Loyola Marymount, one beautiful young woman after another.

Brendan explained why they came, and the Chief bums-rushed him into his private office and shut the door. "Hey, how about me. I brought him in," Wendel said for no one to hear. Myrna walked off to do something, giving Wendel an opportunity to look for his computers. Maybe he'd lift one, though he couldn't very well carry it on his bike. He saw a file marked "Handler" on the assistant's desk and shuffled through it, finding transcribed statements of his neighbors. He was half way through Gorman's statement, reading about how much he, Wendel, was a son-of-a-bitch when the Chief's door opened.

"What the hell do you think you're doing?"

"Proof reading. Your girl made some typos."

"I ought to lock you up."

"With Brendan?"

"Brendan's free to go."

"How about locking me up with my computers for a few hours."

"I sent them to the FBI."

"I could have helped you. I've already read Handler's email and you'll be waiting for weeks to hear from the FBI."

"Get the hell out of here before I charge you with tampering. A felony. San Quentin."

Brendan put his arm across Wendel's shoulder and steered him toward the door. For a moment he wondered what the FBI would make of the two-day date switch on the Dell, but then he spun away from Brendan and said, "Someone's following me. Is that your guy?"

"What makes you think someone's following you?"

After Wendel explained his trip south, the Chief said, "Sounds like your imagination, someone who works at that company who was driving by when you left home."

Outside they walked to Starbucks where, while waiting in line, Brendan suggested that Wendel stop provoking the Chief. When Wendel asked how Brendan walked out so easily, Brendan explained that he had told the Chief the whole story. That it's always easiest to tell the truth because all you have to do is remember what happened. When you lie, you have to remember what hasn't happened.

"I guess it's easy to forget what hasn't happened," Wendel said.

"If you have to lie," Brendan said, "make it simple and as close to the truth as possible. Like one day I got caught AWOL, coming back to the base after an all-nighter with a chick across the bay, so I told them I missed the last ferry and these people were nice enough to put me up. The who and where were all the truth, everything but the intent that they couldn't prove."

"Thanks for the tip," Wendel said, "but I never lie."

Brendan smiled and asked Wendel to tell him about Handler. As Wendel talked, he found telling stories about his friend eased some stress he was carrying—his shoulders sank—which reminded him how obsessed he had become. They laughed over an incident from a few years back when Wendel was in Handler's Paris gallery and a gypsy walked in. Shortly she engaged Wendel in a conversation and guided him over to a painting she liked. As she was about to walk out, Handler stopped her and pulled Wendel's wallet out of her pocket. "Handler invited her to have lunch with us because Gypsies sometimes deal in stolen art and he wanted to learn how they marketed hot items."

"Maybe he was using his knowledge on your painting," Brendan said.

"My painting's not worth anything."

"The Killer might not have known that."

Wendel thought this over. Handler had contacted both Burgher in Switzerland and Victor whatever in Salinas about the painting, so Handler must have thought it was at least unusual. But Burgher thought it was a fake and Victor was just getting around to calling Handler back, so they weren't likely suspects. Maybe Handler talked with someone else.

Wendel told Brendan about the security problem he needed to solve at GeTechNome and asked if Brendan had ever dealt with encryption while he was in the Seals.

"All the time. I doubt if anyone cared about most of the messages we sent, but we encrypted everything."

"Any ideas for my problem. It's kind of like trying to outfox myself. If I come up with a solution, I can probably beat it and break into the system."

"Use an elaborate de-coding key," Brendan said. "Powerful computers that run trial and error solutions at unbelievable speed obsolete everything we used twenty years ago. But the same computers allow you to build and employ de-coding keys that are unbelievably difficult for any computer to break."

"How do I build a de-coding key?"

"I don't know but first you need to check with a lawyer because some encryption use is illegal. Uncle doesn't want to make life easier for terrorists."

"Typical. Pass a law to keep the terrorists from doing something illegal."

They refilled their coffees and split another scone. Five people were working their laptops using Starbuck's wireless hookups, making Wendel wonder if he could get any work done in a place like this. It seemed like every other person who walked in was a female with skin exposed three inches above and below her belly button. He'd never get anything done.

"You plan to get back together with those survivalists?" Wendel asked.

"One of them knows a neighbor of yours," Brendan said.

"A biker and one of my neighbors?" Brendan described a medium height, balding retirement-aged man, and Wendel said, "That's half the old farts on the block."

"Three houses down from you."

"Gorman, a friend of a biker?" Hallelujah, a redeeming feature for Gorman, knowing a whacky survivalist. Maybe someone Gorman hired to kill Wendel. "Which biker?"

"One we call the 'Hammer,'" Brendan said.

"When will you see him again?"

"Later in the month."

"How about taking me along."

"They won't have much patience for your usual irreverence. Think you can control yourself?"

Not really, Wendel thought, but he didn't see any way to avoid the risk if he wanted to pursue the bikers' involvement in Handler's death and perhaps the painting. He could hone his government-bashing, work on self-restraint, and stay close to Brendan. They agreed on the week following Wendel's presentation of his security system to the GeTechNome scientists.

Before going home he dropped into the Internet cafe down the block to pick up his emails. He found only spam, which he didn't filter out; otherwise his mailbox would be empty most days, which always reminded him that he didn't have many friends. Really any friends except for bikers he saw once in a while and people like Handler with whom he got together occasionally after meeting in some business connection. The spam didn't solve his loneliness. Sometimes he considered giving up his consulting business to start a friends-for-people-without-friends web site. He once mentioned this to Margo who said, "You mean a chat room," a subtle putdown that dampened his enthusiasm. He thought about writing his third cousin in St. Louis but couldn't remember his email address, wouldn't know what to say after not communicating for several years and had never really liked the guy. Besides he needed to get home and call Victor in Salinas.

7

"Your Mr. Handler asked if I could help find the original of a Klee print," Zvolens said after Wendell reached him.

Wendell explained that the print was his and how he had returned home from vacation and found Handler dead. He listened carefully because Zvolens' innocent-sounding phone message might have been a cover-up for having killed Handler and stolen the painting.

"I'm not totally surprised," Zvolens said.

"That's striking. Why not?"

"This painting, was it a silk screen?"

"Handler contacted someone in Switzerland who told him it probably wasn't a Klee. But you didn't explain why you're not surprised someone killed him. Murders in my house don't usually happen in odd years."

"He contacted me and he contacted the Swiss. Who knows whom else he might have told about this unusual Klee painting."

"Even if it's a fake."

"Perhaps it's not a fake," Zvolens said. "Klee was an innovator. He produced so many pieces of art we undoubtedly aren't aware of them all. Curators learn about new items even now. Any chance of bringing it up for me to take a look?"

"I wish I could." He explained how the Klee was the only thing missing from his house when he got home.

"Of course it's missing," Zvolens said. "How about sending me a picture?"

"Better yet, how about if I bring one up? You have me interested, and I'd like to learn more about Klee." And he wanted to learn about Mr. Zvolens.

Wendel was so pleased with this development that not until they made a date for the following Wednesday did he realize he had no photo of the Klee. But Handler had taken one. All he had to do was get back onto a computer and find it. He called Cheryl and asked if he could use hers. She said sure and suggested they follow up with a hot tub. "The sun's behind the jacaranda tree and we'll be in the shade."

Wendel's email account was still blocked. He could probably break into his server, but none of the servers appreciated intrusions. Several had hired him to break in as a test of their security. He strained to recall the name of the person Handler had emailed the picture but couldn't come up with it.

"Let's do the tub and maybe you'll remember," Cheryl said as she watched over his shoulder.

"More likely I'll fall asleep," he said.

"That's what it's for, to relax."

He followed her outside and they both tossed their clothes on a rack she kept next to the tub. Wendel was certain he'd been naked with Cheryl more often than her ex had, probably twice as often. She had a great body—slight tummy, moderate-sized firm breasts that had never mothered—which he thought he had gotten used to enjoying without ogling. When every once in a while she caught him looking, she smiled and gave him a gentle crotch rub with the ball of her foot. "Up periscope," she liked to say. Implicitly their relationship was platonic. Not that there was no sexual tension, at least for Wendel. He figured he was saving sex with Cheryl for the proverbial "rainy day," and liked to assume that she felt the same way.

"Your tub never smells of chlorine," he said.

"Never use it. I'm clean."

""How about your guests."

"Like you?"

"Like the studs."

She waved him off as though it wasn't worth answering. Wendel lay back and watched a chickadee flit in and out of the jacaranda. He loved the hot tub, especially not having to take care of it, and was delighted there was no chlorine smell.

"What's going on with the police?" she asked.

"Stumble, stumble," he said. "They haven't a clue would be my guess."

"Your painting?"

"No idea. I'm sure whoever killed Handler wanted the Klee."

"Not necessarily," she said.

For a moment he was surprised she had an opinion about the stolen painting, surprised that she even thought about it. Yet he knew Cheryl had the smarts that might have landed her in upper management if she had been born ten years later. "Who else would have it?" he said.

"A couple times Handler said the painting fascinated him. Almost like it was more of a Klee than a Klee, I think he said. Maybe he did something with it."

"He wouldn't have stolen my art no matter how interested he was."

"I don't mean steal it. Maybe he gave it to someone to study, thinking he'd get it back before you returned."

Wendel thought it over. He recalled the Chief telling him that Handler's office thought he was in California on business. If Cheryl were right, whoever had it would return it, unless they thought it was valuable and figured with Handler dead, who would know. He recalled Zvolens asking who else had Handler called. "Maybe the killer doesn't have it," Wendel said, "but I think most likely he does. I can't get the murder out of my head, like in a way I'm responsible and I'm obsessed with finding him. If he took the Klee, maybe the Klee will lead me to him."

"Who are your suspects?" Cheryl said.

"Burgher. That's it, the name I couldn't remember." Wendel stood up dripping water.

"Who?"

"Burgher's the guy Handler sent the picture to at the Klee something-or-other in Lucerne. I'll get a copy from his email."

Sitting in his wet boxers at Cheryl's desk, Wendel googled Burgher, Klee and Lucerne and quickly came up with Der Klee Entwurf. He assumed that "praesident" next to Burgher's name meant he was in charge. He made a move on the site and immediately wished he hadn't when he encountered more than rudimentary security. He'd have to break through and was certain he had already alerted the Entwurf to track the intrusion back to Cheryl's computer. He told her and apologized. To help he went next door and returned with a utility he had written that would allow him to encroach further under the appearance of other users, all fictional but made to appear that the owner was covered by camouflage. Theoretically the Entwurf would think that Cheryl was just another site that some hacker was hiding behind.

After spreading this ground fog, Wendel set to work again trying to enter Burgher's email, finding the task harder than he suspected. He inserted a second utility he had brought that would try an endless progression of passwords. A half hour later he was in, though additional security protected certain folders. The Handler email was readily available with the picture intact. He was tempted to break into the guarded folders to see what the Entwurf considered so secret, but he had already violated his own principles against cyber snooping, so he grabbed the picture and got out.

"Do you have a color printer?" he asked Cheryl who was standing behind him watching.

"I don't. Remind me, by the way, not to put any secrets on this damn computer with stalkers like you lurking around."

"You're reminded. Normally—," he started to explain to her, but decided talking about his lofty principles would sound hollow. "I'll save this on my flash storage, get it off your computer, and cover my tracks best I can."

When he finished, she said, "When I have color to print, Henry Gorman does it for me. He's got all kinds of equipment."

"Make my day. Ask Gorman for a favor?"

"Don't forget, he's sucking up right now."

"Want to walk down with me?"

"I have to pack for a weekend workshop at Esalen. My accountant says I need to either change my life style or find a rich man."

"Why Esalen?"

"A yoga workshop plus old guys with money. A two-for."

Wendel hated to ask Gorman for anything, but he didn't want to drive to Long Beach for a printing service. When he phoned, the great man said to come right over. Would Wendel like some red or white wine waiting when he got there? Wendel pulled out his flash storage and walked up the lane, wondering if Gorman was an alcoholic. He thought he had read somewhere that addictions went along with quests for power and control.

Gorman greeted him with a glass of Chardonnay and gestured him toward one of two great rooms branching off the entry hall. The other great room, he could see as he walked past, housed large sitting and dining areas. The walls of each were covered with what looked like expensive art, including several that looked, in Wendel's quick glimpse, like Klee-era surrealism. Gorman led him into a large living room with no art on the circular wall, but instead featuring a grand piano and an upright piano. "Sometimes Gloria and I do double concertos," Gorman said, "and Gloria hates the grand." He pushed a button that made a part of the wall recede into the adjacent paneling, revealing an office alcove with a desk and an iMac.

Wendel went to work and shortly displayed the Klee on the 24-inch screen.

"Colorful," Gorman said. "It's hooked up to the color printer. Go ahead. Mind making me one? I like it."

Of course Wendel minded but what could he do? Gorman's desire for the copy suggested he hadn't stolen the painting; otherwise he could make his own picture. But maybe asking for the picture was a facade.

"Would you like a larger version?" Gorman said. I have a machine that will do that." Without waiting for an answer, he walked his copy across the room, pushed another button that opened another alcove containing a large apparatus like Wendel had seen in an architect's office. Damned if he didn't produce a copy very close to the size of Wendel's lost painting.

"You have an entire print shop," he said.

"When you sell your business, you have to do something with your money. I'll show you more." Gorman opened a small window in the panel exposing a touch pad on which he tapped a combination that caused a section of the panel, twice as large as the alcove openings, to recede into the wall. Wendell was ready for an Imax movie. Instead Gorman exposed a gun collection the size you might encounter in a museum, twenty or so rifles or what looked to Wendel, a greenhorn, like automatic rifles, plus an assortment of pistols.

"Impressive," Wendel said trying not to show surprise or alarm or whatever the hell he was feeling. Is he sending me a message, he wondered? Not that he needed to. Wendel figured that Gorman, who could hire his own private police force to patrol the neighborhood, could find a way to deal with him like someone dealt with Handler if that were his intention. He was probably safe, from Gorman at least, as long as he was considering Gorman's proposition to join the club. "You could hold off a battalion. Do you hunt or just collect?"

"My company made all these guns while I owned it. I've done some hunting, but now I'm into paintball. Have you ever done that?"

"I keep a shotgun and a 38 for protection," he lied hoping to make Gorman think twice if he thought about intruding. "Fortunately I've never had to use them."

"You ought to join us some day. It's like playing games we used to play as kids. You ever play 'guns.'"

Wendel had. He'd even had bean-shooter fights before the EPA or some other federal agency banned them, but he didn't want to encourage Gorman, so he said no.

"You're not a gun-control guy, are you?" Gorman asked.

"I'm not an anything-control guy," Wendel said, wondering if Gorman had heard his lie about the two guns he supposedly had.

"I should have guessed," Gorman said.

"You can't control guns any more than booze, drugs, sex, and neighbors."

"Touche." Gorman was quiet, maybe conflicted over his need to control just about everything and his intuition that Wendel was right. Sooner or later some asshole like Gorman would become president and decide the country couldn't do without him, so he'd declare martial law at the end of his term. It wouldn't work. Even in China and Russia it eventually didn't work.

Wendel thanked him for the prints and added that he was swamped just getting back from vacation but would consider the gate in a week or two.

"As long as the guards can stay, take your time," Gorman said in a voice that reminded Wendel of his father making it clear that he would get his way and that further discussion would be futile.

Wendel would take his time. And meanwhile he had a picture to show Zvolens on what should be an interesting trip.

8

The next day the Chief dropped by around two in the afternoon. At the door Wendel said, "Did you bring my computers?"

"You better buy a new one," the Chief said.

Actually he was pleased not to have a computer at the moment. Between Cheryl, Gorman and GeTechNome he had access, and kind of enjoyed not sitting in front of the damn thing. Probably his imagination but he seemed more creative without a computer than with one when he considered the security issues at GeTechNome.

"Odor's a little better," the Chief said as he walked in without an invitation.

Wendel thanked him for the ozonator tip and asked what he needed.

"We picked up 28 different sets of prints in your house, 22 identifiable. Tell me who these people are." He pulled a list of names out of his pocket and handed it to Wendel.

Many Wendel didn't know. "Bikers bring their friends and I don't catch their names. Johnson I know because he plays the guitar. And Martin helped me pick out my bike. They both come around from time to time."

Then he saw Margo's name and about dropped the list, surprised not only that her prints were around after almost 20 years, but also that the FBI had a match on file.

"Margo's my ex-wife."

"You mentioned that the other night. You sure she hasn't been out here since the divorce?"

"Maybe back when our daughter was in town. I don't remember. How long do prints last?"

"When was that?"

"When was what?"

"Your daughter in town."

"At least 5 years ago."

"How long you been divorced?"

"Almost 20 years."

"They can last forever, but some of these are too fresh for five years and some are from surfaces that even a bachelor can't help but smear or wipe up like the counter-top in your bathroom. Think back and tell me when she was last here."

Wendel had no trouble looking like he was thinking, not about when Margo was there last, but about what the hell she was doing in his bathroom. He finally shrugged and said I can't remember another time, but I'll ask her if you want."

"I'll take care of that," the Chief said.

After he left, Wendel called Margo about getting together to meet her husband about the consulting job and to get her advice on buying an espresso maker. Later she called back to confirm next Monday, a couple days before he was meeting Victor Zvolens in Salinas.

Home for less than a week, his obsession with Handler's murder had him ready for another vacation. Between

Margo's prints, Gorman's guns, Brendan's helmet, Burgher in Switzerland, and Zvolens in Salinas, questions hummed in and out of his unfocused mind at a rate that left no room or time for answers. Besides he wanted to think through GeTechNome security issues but his creativity would work best if he went somewhere he'd never been before, where his senses and brain were more alert.

After a swim at the beach and a dose of Cheryl's hot tub, alone, which made him feel lonely, he wheeled his Kawasaki out of the garage and took off for he knew not where. Friday rush hour traffic was still heavy so he kept to the back roads, found a dive for dinner and then headed north to Ojai and a biker-bar he'd been to before.

"Wendel," he said holding out his hand to a man he knew only by sight.

"Sure, I remember. I'm Gums," the man answered, and then Wendel recalled that Gums took his teeth out at night. At the moment he was nursing a beer and jawing with the matron when she wasn't pouring drafts and pitchers for the tables.

Wendel ordered a Leininkugels, which he knew they wouldn't have—one day he'd find a Leinys outside of Wisconsin—and settled for a Bud. After a couple of beers and a game of shuffleboard, Gums said some bikers were getting together in Pozo on Saturday.

"Do you know the Hammer?" Wendel asked.

"How could you not," Gums said. "He's not around that much but if he is, just listen for the loudest."

"Is he going to Pozo?"

"Could be, though he lives up north."

The end-of-summer weather was perfect for camping under the stars in a field a little out of town, where the rising sun got him off to an early start. Back roads and mountain paths north of Santa Barbara gave him a chance to take advantage of the Kawasaki's suspension system. At a pass in the Santa Ynez Mountains his phone confirmed what he already knew, that he had no reception and was out of touch with the world. A feeling of vulnerable aloneness sent a shiver of excitement through his body. He was fearful and thrilled, more accurately terrified and ecstatic. Alone as he would be at death, yet able to surmount his fear, or more accurately get through his fear for the moment.

In the mountains north of Foxen Canyon Road he flew over a ridge and landed fifty yards in front of a mountain lion. To his relief the lion was backing away, like it might turn and run. Still Wendel braked too hard, fishtailed, and skidded to a stop, the last few feet smashing his leg against the rocks. Ahead he looked into the eyes of a bloody dead animal the cougar had been chewing, probably a rabbit with long ears. Wendel's jeans were damp. His leg was bleeding. As he crawled out from under the bike, the cat turned and slowly walked in his direction. Wendel pictured the rabbit as an appetizer and himself the main course.

The rabbit was less than a hundred feet away. He wanted to move back, give the cat some room. Without a running start they could leap forty feet. But Wendel knew retreating from a mountain lion was an invitation. Instead he stood tall as he could, arms raised in the air to make him look larger. His brain raced for an option in case this didn't scare off the cougar. Throwing rocks or raising the bike and rolling it at the charging cat would be futile. He would have no options other than to fight the animal.

How the hell would he do that? He better hit him hard with a rock or he'd be cat food. At best the animal would leave him terribly wounded in a place without phone service. Before he could think more, the cat took a slow arrogant step in his direction. Sharp nails at the end of its claws gripped the loose terrain. Slowly Wendel knelt and grabbed a fist-sized rock. The cat opened its mouth like he was about to roar. Gaping jaws revealed huge lower incisors. Its roar was not a roar but sounded like a human scream that sent chills down Wendel's back. When the cat took another step, Wendel wanted to run. But he didn't. One more step and the cougar scooped up the rabbit, turned and walked off.

Wendel sank to the ground, aware of his racing heart, and watched the mountain lion disappear over another ridge. For long moments he sat as the adrenaline ebbed and calmness returned. He had been lucky. Riding back-country alone had its obvious dangers, a challenge he consciously accepted. He had an unwarranted conceit he could handle great risks. The challenge and the danger turned him on. It was worth it. The same attitude was probably responsible for his looking for Handler's killer and the missing phony Klee. He realized as his thoughts wandered away from the cougar that ego drove him to retrieve the painting because it represented a story, part of the tale of the life of Wendel, a story that would be distinct from the tales that made up most peoples' lives.

His pants were torn and a one-inch wound on his leg was still bleeding though not heavily. When he retrieved the first-aid kit from the bike, he discovered the rocks had torn his front tire as well, leaving an obvious gash and the tire flat. He cleaned the wound with water and a washrag he kept with the kit because this was not his first accident. He might need some stitches but he'd have to settle for a pressure bandage for now. First he applied antibiotic ointment and gauze. Then the tape.

Before he met Brendan, Wendel traveled only main roads because he didn't know how to handle repairs. Brendan took him into the hills and made him practice, so that if it weren't for the wound that throbbed under the tape, he'd welcome the refresher course. The rip in the tire was larger than any he had ever repaired. He realized that if he couldn't get the job done, he could wait years for help. He cleaned the gash and then used the sharpened end of the tire iron he carried to rough up the surfaces. The end of the iron also worked to spread some glue. Carefully he prepared a plug and added cement. After inserting the plug, and waiting for the cement to dry, he used a CO_2 cartridge to add enough air to test the repair by spitting and looking for bubbles. None, so he filled up the tire.

By the time he reached Lopez Lake, his leg felt better so he continued on to Pozo rather than back to civilization and a doctor. A parking place beckoned next to a bike with an Idaho plate that read "Hammer."

9

A crew of bikers looked well into a liquid afternoon when he entered the tavern a little after three. Gums and several other men many of whom had been at Wendel's house one time or another sat along with a good-sized group at some tables in a corner. He ordered a beer and pulled up a chair. Brendan sometimes talked about the one-percenters, the old-time Hells-Angels-type bikers who thought they ought to be running the world. Not this group of adventure cyclists, guys like Wendel riding bikes with good suspension, effective mufflers, and side bags the one-percenters would ridicule.

Conversation was about the nascent football season, fantasy teams in fantasy leagues they competed in, kids off to college, even the weather and how lack of rain made the trails so dry. Wendel listened, not particularly interested, yet comfortable to have a respite from the solitude that both soothed and upset him. A man moved his chair over next to Wendel and reminded him that his name was Jamie.

"Where you been? Haven't seen you for a while," Jamie said.

"Vacation. Getting back in the groove. Feels good to get out."

"Looks like you took a spill." Jamie pointed to the stained jeans, which stirred Wendel to pull up the pant leg. No fresh blood had soaked through the bandage, but now that he turned his attention to it, he felt it throb. He told Jamie about his encounter with the cougar.

"I never ride alone in the mountains," Jamie said.

"You're smarter than I am."

"I enjoyed meeting your friend last week or was it a week before," Jamie said.

"Not sure who you're talking about," Wendel said.

"The fella staying at your house."

"Do you remember when you dropped by?" Wendel's interest rose wondering how close to Handler's murder Jamie's visit had been by.

"Was he a Frog or a Kraut?" Jamie said.

"A little of each. Were you over on Sunday?"

"Yeah, the Sunday before last. Nice of you to let your buddy ride your bike. I don't know if I'd have done that."

"I didn't know," Wendel said. "What happened?"

"Hey, three more pitchers," called out one of the men Wendel could tell fancied himself as a leader, reminding Wendel of Gorman, his neighbor. "Make it four," the man said.

"Hey Wendel," yelled another man. "Where you been all day? Trying to get us drunk before we play poker."

"Turn on the Cal game," said the Gorman-type to the bartender. "Get rid of that Big Ten flag football."

"Screw Cal. USC is on ESPN," someone else said.

"I didn't know Handler, my friend, was out biking. Tell me about it."

"A bunch of guys were over at your house. Brendan came with the guy who's ordering the beer, introduced him as the 'Hammer,' said he was a survivalist. I didn't know you needed to be an asshole to survive," said Jamie. Wendel watched the Hammer—what a name—pick up two pitchers and put one down on their table. "Thanks," they both said as the Hammer walked away. "Brendan went for food and never came back. Called up and said he had an emergency. So we all drove out to the In 'n Out Burger. Your buddy rode your bike. Real well, like he rode all the time. He and the Hammer ended up in a conversation and the two of them stayed after the rest of us took off."

Wendel watched the Hammer carry two more pitchers from the bar to the tables, announcing that everyone should drink up. Then he started an argument with the guy who wanted the USC game, told him to fuck off. Wendel had met all kinds of people in the biker world. Guys running zillion-dollar businesses, ultimate fighters, pacifists, suit-and-tie corporate types, even an occasional housewife and one househusband, whose wife gave him a weekend off a month to ride his motorcycle. If Wendel didn't know the Hammer was a north-woods survivalist, he'd have guessed he was a prof at UC-Berkeley or for that matter, a Berkeley hair stylist, playing tough guy on weekends, perhaps out wearing his wife's underwear. He wondered where Brendan met the guy.

Wendel went to take a leak and get his thoughts together. What had Handler and the Hammer found of interest to discuss? Wendel had never known Handler to care about politics and doubted that he had any idea about the American survivalist persona. Wendel wished he knew more about Handler.

Back inside he excused himself to Jamie and dragged his chair over to the Hammer's table and introduced himself.

"What's your fuckup, Wendel," the Hammer said.

"Computers. I write software. If you've got a computer you know there's plenty of fuckups."

"I've got a computer to keep track of the government." He laughed. "What do you think of that, keeping track of the government."

"I guess turnaround's fair play." Wendel sometimes thought about breaking into the government's most secret files. The NSA supposedly collected volumes of data all around the world. He could do it and maybe cover his tracks. Maybe not. He guessed the NSA employed a team of Wendels who would try to track him down. Besides he had no interest in breeching the government's snooping branch. The FBI on the other hand probably had all kinds of information they shouldn't have, so that if he got his hands on it, they'd never prosecute him for fear of being exposed.

"Damn fucking right it's fair play," the Hammer said. "Stay ahead of them suckers or they'll do you in."

"I wanted to ask you about a friend of mine," Wendel said. "You were at my house with some of the guys a couple weeks ago, south of LA. I was out of town but my friend, Handler, went off for a ride with you."

"Don't recall."

"The day you were riding with Brendan Wilde."

"Oh yeah. That Brendan's a guy."

"Handler was living in my house. Rode my Kawasaki. The same street where your buddy Gorman lives."

"Your leg doesn't look so good. Let me take a look."

Before Wendel could answer, the Hammer bent down and pulled up the pant leg. The blood had soaked through the bandage, so Wendel peeled back the tape to check out the wound.

"Hold on," the Hammer said. "Let's put something fresh on," and he got up and walked out the door. Two minutes later he returned with a first aid kit, applied fresh ointment and a clean pack, while Wendel tried to figure out the combination of aggression and kindness. When he tore off the tape from the spool, he said, "What were you saying about the guy at your house?"

"Many thanks," Wendel said as he felt around the bandage to test for pain. "When I got home last week, Handler was dead in the front hall." Wendel watched for a reaction and saw none. "I'm wondering if he might have said something that would be a clue as to why."

The Hammer sat and stared at the TV someone had switched to USC-Oregon State, a better game because USC was struggling in the rain in Eugene.

"You mean like a heart condition he might have talked about."

"Actually someone shot him. In the head. Up close."

Without a pause, the Hammer said, "It's a violent world."

"He didn't mention any trouble he was in? You might have been one of the last people to see him alive."

"You working with the police? I don't answer police questions."

"No, but he was a friend. And it looks like whoever shot him took a painting of mine." Wendel again watched closely for a reaction and thought he saw a sudden small twitch of the head at the mention of the Klee.

"He did tell me about a painting. Thought I might be interested because it's by a German."

"I don't get it," Wendel said. "Germans love the government. You hate the government. "

"Especially when some bad ass takes over. Maybe your friend thought I want to take over the government."

Wendel waited for more, but the Hammer was back into TV and football. "Thanks again," Wendel said. "Need another pitcher?"

"Too late. I have to wheel out of here.'

"By the way, what makes you a Cal fan?"

"Nothing really. But I like to let these guys know who's in charge. He flashed a brief smile and then yelled, "Hey turn the Cal game back on."

IO

Monday morning Wendel left early not wanting to be late for Margo, irritated and perplexed that she could still provoke his anxiety. Characteristically slow traffic on the 405 left him immersed in a Margo memory that reassured him he had been only half-crazy to marry her. The Sixties didn't reach his part of the Midwest until the decade was almost over—for Wendel an orgy still meant kissing girls on New Years Eve. At his first such party after returning from Viet Nam, Margo was the only young woman who played tongue tag. Courtship was frantic, romance and sex overshadowing flaws. They got married on Valentines Day. Ten minutes before they traded vows, she had cursed her swollen feet and thrown her shoes at him, ten minutes later walking down the aisle barefoot, charming guests, first with her boldness and later with tales of the minister's lecture about disrespect.

His Margo anxieties provoked the memory of their honeymoon driving from San Francisco to Los Angeles on Highway 1. In Carmel, Margo wanted to stay in a hotel that cost more for a night than they planned to spend the next week. Wendel said no. Margo checked in anyway—this was before hotels requested a credit cart at registration—and Wendel slept in the car. When he refused to write a check in the morning, she began a tantrum on the street: "Pay the hotel or I'll have the police put you in jail," she screamed. "You're a cheap, cold, thoughtless liar. No wonder no one else would marry you. I should have known." She threw the coffee cup she had carried from breakfast at him, leaving a bruise on his forehead and a wet stain on his shirt.

Wendel walked into the hotel and up to the front desk. Guests who had been drawn out to the porch gathered inside the door where Margo stood and watched.

"My wife spends money we can't afford," he said. "I refused to stay here because I knew we couldn't pay the bill. You'll have to collect from her."

The clerk fetched a manager. Wendel repeated the story. "Just leave," the manager said in a calm voice. "Our security guard will accompany you to your room to get your belongings," he said to Margo. She refused to go, so Wendel followed the guard while Margo screamed that she'd call the police if he touched her things.

By noon she was talking and joking as though nothing had happened, even laughing about the hotel manager's lisp that Wendel hadn't even heard. Meanwhile Wendel walked on egg shells for the rest of the trip, afraid of provoking her temper, which stormed throughout their marriage, usually without provocation.

Margo was waiting at the ground-floor entrance to the Design Center, reading some papers and impatiently looking up and down Melrose. "You're late," she said after he crossed the street and they exchanged a brush of cheeks.

"Five minutes," he said. "Within the L.A. grace period."

"Forget the grace period if you're going to work for Howard."

Wendel congratulated himself that he had spent 25 years avoiding the Howards of the world and rued that because of his finances he now might need them.

"What's the limp?" Margo said as they walked to the Design Cafe.

"A minor motorcycle incident." He was unaware he was limping even though his leg hurt. The wound was doing okay, but his thigh was swollen and black and blue.

"Great jacket," Margo said with a trace of sarcasm.

"You bought it for me."

"For your thirtieth birthday. You still driving that old car?"

"Old is beautiful," he said a bit too defensively.

"It can be," she said, but her tone of voice showed that she didn't believe his jacket and car were proof.

"I appreciate your recommending me to your husband."

"You always were good at computers."

She omitted her old refrain, "and good for nothing else." The only useful advice Wendel's shrink had given him was that he wouldn't give up Margo until he first figured out why he had married her. Some answers were easy: her intuitive good taste and spontaneity, the same qualities that now made her the successful editor-in-chief of a best-selling design magazine. What took him eight years to understand was why he stayed married to someone who buried him with criticism and rage. Eventually he had realized she made it unnecessary for him to initiate conflict, which he hated to do. "Passive-aggressive," the shrink later told him. As long as Margo picked the fights he didn't have to give up his self-image that he was the nice guy. She de-pacified his anger by unleashing it, as she was about to do right now, yet for the moment he held his tongue. He wanted the consulting project, wanted her help finding an espresso maker, and mostly wanted to learn how her fresh fingerprints had turned up in his house.

"You've certainly found your niche in the publishing world," he said.

"More than a niche. Howard talks about my taking over his empire so he can play."

"You're good at running things."

"Too bad you didn't realize that sooner."

Why did people who ran things have to be such ass holes, he wanted to say, but they had reached the cafe so instead he asked what she wanted to order. With their drinks at a table, his thoughts wandered while Margo explained how she had begun a fashion magazine in addition to the design magazine and how she had come up with a new A-line skirt that was setting a pattern for the winter season and Christmas sales.

"Damn. They fucked it up she said as she rose from her chair. Back she went with her mocha to the counter where she pushed to the front of the line to right whatever wrong the woman working there had inflicted on her drink.

Wendel watched her and listened to two guys across the room loudly debate some decision made by the Dodgers' manager. At the next table, four women in prim business attire—suits and conservative blouses, which seemed out of place in LA—discussed the proper amount of sage and marjoram in homemade tomato soup. He wondered if men were genetically wired to talk sports and women cooking. Except for soccer, which few men cared about, at least in this country, he preferred soup to sports.

Margo returned with a new mocha while people in line stared after her, though none had challenged her chutzpa. "Those guys are right about the Dodgers'," she said. "I could do a better job."

She gave him the name and number of her husband's secretary to call to arrange a meeting on the consulting gig, and directed him to a couple of stores down Melrose for the espresso maker. With that information in hand, Wendel said, "Did you read the story in the Times about Handler's murder?"

"It's all dreadful," she said in a voice that sounded a little lower. "What have you heard from the police?"

"My life's been on hold," Wendel said. "The police coming and going. Gorman—don't know if you knew him—hiring guards to protect the street, fans all over my house because Handler had been dead a few days when I got home. Have you ever heard of an ozonator?"

"I ran an article on removing house odors. I know all about ozonators." When she raised her mocha, her hand shook slightly. Behind him, the women were quiet at the next table. When he turned to see if they had left, they glanced away, caught listening to the murder story. Oh well. He'd be doing the same.

"Friday the Chief of police shows up and shows me a list of people whose fingerprints they found in the house. Including yours." This time Margo folded her left leg over her right, which wasn't so easy sitting at the table.

"I didn't know fingerprints stayed around so long," she said in a quiet voice they couldn't hear at the next table. "Let's go for a walk." She led him from the cafe, outside to an esplanade that ran down and around a long reflecting pool with a fountain.

"Some of the prints were fresh, like when were you recently in my bathroom?" He heard the accusatory edge in his voice and expected Margo to explode. But she didn't. Instead she looked down and walked on. For Margo, always the aggressor, her demeanor was defensive, a reaction he couldn't recall from their past.

"Look, it was harmless," she said. "I called when you were out of town about the I.T. consulting opportunity, and Jean answered."

"Jean? I thought it was John."

"It is. We talked for a while and then he invited me out. Said you had acquired some contemporary art, which he thought would be interesting to see. I probably got my prints all over including in the bathroom which I used."

"I think you saw my art when Kate was in town a few years ago." Wendel enjoyed interrogating Margo, Margo back on her heels. He was on a roll.

"I wasn't really thinking. Jean...Handler caught me by surprise when he answered the phone. I had to run down to Newport Beach for a house tour so I dropped by."

"Something's funny here," he said. "It's not like one or two fingerprints around the doorbell." He didn't know how many prints or where else the police had found them, but his intuition pushed him on. "You'd be better off contacting the police before they chase you down. If your story doesn't make sense, they'll see you as a suspect."

"Hell," she said and stopped walking. She turned to him, uncertainty, maybe even fear, in her face. "There was no house tour. I shacked up with Handler all afternoon."

"In my house," he said in a voice he didn't think he had.

"Yes in our house. I can't believe you have the same bed we used to share."

"Sharing it was easy to forget so I flipped the mattress and started over." His voice lacked his usual defensive tone in response to Margo's criticism. She reacted by letting out a breath and seemed to shrink right on the sidewalk.

"What'll I do?" she said.

"Call Chief Pruett. Tell him the whole story."

"What about Howard? If he learns I fucked that Kraut-Frog, I'll have a problem."

"I doubt if the Chief's interested in whom you fuck or in Howard for that matter. Unless Howard learned about it. Then maybe he killed Handler. Or if Handler threatened you with blackmail, maybe you killed him."

Margo pressed her lips together and he knew from eight years of marriage that she was also gritting if not grinding her teeth, a habit she hadn't overcome despite her dentist's warnings. All at once Wendel felt bad at how much he was enjoying her discomfort. Enjoying it so much that he was losing track of learning some important information.

"When were you there?" he said.

"I don't know," she almost mumbled, her mind elsewhere he could tell.

"A weekend? A Wednesday? Can you remember the day?"

"Who are you, the police?" she said, regaining some composure.

"I'm trying to focus you on questions the police will ask."

She started walking again and he fell in beside her. "A Monday afternoon," she said. "There was a house tour I didn't care about. Howard was in New York. I'm sure he fucks everything in sight when he travels, so I figured why not me one time."

"Howard might not care if he finds out about you and Handler."

"He'd care," she said. "You don't understand alpha males."

She was right. Wendel pictured some elephant seals he had watched one day when traveling up the coast. An alpha male with 20 or so females, savagely chased off another male even though Wendel would have thought the alpha could use a little help servicing a harem like that.

"You're in a spot," he said. "Any way I can help I will. The police might know the date of death by now, so you might think about where you were and who you were with the past two weeks."

"Thanks," she said. "I have an eleven o'clock and better get back. Don't forget to give Howard a call."

"One more thing. Did Handler say anything about my Klee picture? It was the only thing missing from the house."

"He said that old copy was worth at least five million dollars, or something like that."

"A copy worth five million. I guess that got your attention."

"He was talking about the original, sweetheart, not that piece of junk."

"That piece of junk might be worth millions. What else did he say about it?"

"I paid more attention when he said that looking at me next to the Klee with all its scarlet provoked his passion beyond his resistance. I wouldn't take it too seriously. You know the French."

She turned to leave, but Wendel said, "Margo," and she turned back. "You had no business fucking...anyone in my house." He almost added, "It's perverse," but he'd said enough.

"I know. It's something that just happened and I wish it hadn't. But don't be so smug, what with your hermetic lifestyle, motorcycle-gang friends. Now I'm in trouble with the police and maybe my husband all because I called to help you land a consulting project. Think about that."

No brushing of cheeks as she turned and walked off leaving Wendel both contrite and guilty about feeling so good about her predicament. He found the espresso maker but without the joy he had been looking forward to duplicating from his trip. Unlike a minute ago, she was up and he was down. In the end, Margo always controlled the seesaw.

He wanted a restful rest of the day before going to Salinas, but was afraid that the way his life was going, he might not be so lucky.

11

On the way home Wendel stopped at the Apple store in Manhattan Beach to check his emails. Being a computer consultant without a computer appealed to him. Besides the spam in his inbox, the only name he recognized was Sally Simms at GeTechNome, reminding him of his commitment to present a security package to the scientists. Their resistance, she added, was "becoming more militant each day, especially Waldo Peterson whom the others look to for leadership."

As he pondered security at GeTechNome, one of the college kids selling iMacs introduced himself and Betty something-or-other whom he said he was training. He showed Wendel several bells and whistles the iMac could perform. Wendel told them he didn't like how the screensaver rotated different pictures while he preferred only one. After the salesman stumbled around the options before announcing no change was possible, Wendel suggested they use the iMac to take a picture of the screen he wanted, enter the picture into iPhoto, and then make the iPhoto file with only one picture the screensaver. The salesman departed with Betty to impress some other customer, but Betty looked back and winked at Wendel.

Wendel used the iMac's search engine to read about asymmetric cryptography. As he took notes, he wondered if the Department of Homeland Security tracked poten-

tial terrorists by snooping on whoever researched sophisticated cryptography systems. If so he was fortunate that
Chief Pruett had taken his computers so that he was
forced to anonymously use Apple's. Let them come question Betty-what's-her-name whom he noticed across the
room had quite a delectable body.

The guard at the lane to his street was the same one
who stopped him with the Humvee. Today he gave the
forefinger wave.

"They treating you okay?" Wendel asked.

"What do you mean?"

"Some of the residents here treat people like...well
like servants. Anything I can bring you? Like a cup of
coffee?"

"No sir." No smile either.

A yellow Post-It on his front door demanded that
Wendel report immediately to Chief Pruett.

Not "could you give me a call" or "could you drop
by this afternoon." Wendel brooded over distinctions
in wording like that. He responded by changing into his
bathing suit and traipsing across the dune for a swim in
the ocean. Without bothering Cheryl, he basked in her
hot tub, walked home, put some laundry in the washer,
took a shower, clipped his toenails, threw on some jeans
and a sports shirt, and drove down to the village.

"What's up," he said as he knocked on the Chief's
open door.

"That guard tells me you've been home over an hour.
Doing what?"

"I had to wrap up some urgent business. I didn't
think you'd mind."

"What I mind...Sit down. What I mind is you meddling in my investigation. I get a call from you wife and learn you've told her she might be a suspect."

A shudder ran through Wendel's body at the thought of Margo as his wife, making him wonder if desire were as much a part of his feelings as aversion.

"We met because she called me last week about a consulting position with her husband's business. She's my former wife you know."

"What do her fingerprints have to do with your consulting?"

"I asked her if she'd been in my house when I wasn't there."

"Had she?"

"And I asked her about the painting that was stolen. You don't seem very interested in it."

"I doubt someone would kill your friend to steal a painting you bought for three dollars."

"You must know by now that Handler used my computer to email Switzerland about that painting?"

"Right. When was your wife in your house last?"

"And that the painting's a fake."

"You mean a copy," the Chief said. "There is a difference. Your wife was in your house—?"

"Ask her."

"Look Wendel. I'm the police. You're not. If you hadn't been 7000 miles away, you'd be suspect number one. You still might have hired someone to kill Monsieur Handler, so you're still a suspect. What did your wife tell you about being in your house?"

"She said she called me while I was away and Handler answered the phone. She knew him from years before—"

Myrna interrupted him. "Gloria Gorman from Mr. Wendel's street is on the line. Needs to talk to you."

"Tell her I'm busy. I'll call back in a few minutes."

"She says her husband has been murdered."

At least Wendel didn't have to tell the Chief about Margo fucking Handler. The Chief shot out of his chair, grabbed his jacket and was gone like one of those high-octane motorcycles Wendel hated. Before Wendel could get his thoughts together and get out of his own chair, the Chief stuck his head back in the door and said, "You're not 7000 miles away this time. Care to explain what you were doing this morning."

Driving home, Wendel mulled over being a suspect, the Chief's skeptical look when he tried to justify his hour at home after reading the Chief's note on his door. Everyone knew he didn't like Gorman. How plausible was it that after getting the Chief's note, he went for a swim and a hot tub. Just as plausible that he walked down the dune to Gorman's house and shot him, or knifed him, or did whatever it was someone had done to him. He wondered if Cheryl had seen him in the hot tub. Probably not or she would have stuck her head out the window or joined him. Who would have killed Gorman, he asked himself with bewilderment. What the hell was going on with his neighborhood? If he were perverse, he'd suspect some real estate developer was trying to scare everyone into moving.

A dull knife or other crude cutting instrument turned out to be the weapon. A couple hours later the

Chief knocked on his door and asked if he could search the house or whether he should get a warrant and then search the house. Wendel gave his consent, a mistake his lawyer later told him despite Wendel's belief that he had nothing to hide. "They always find something they can use against you," the lawyer would say.

The Chief confiscated all of Wendel's kitchen knives, so dull they couldn't kill anyone. He gave Wendel a list of items he was taking: the knives, some cooking forks, a shears from the garage that he used only when one of his rare surviving plants grew enough to block a window, several pairs of gloves he used when he cycled, even his toenail scissors that could maybe kill a caterpillar, and his motorcycle tools.

"Do you have to take the tools?" he said to the Chief. "I need them when I have an emergency on the road." He didn't see the tire iron with the other items and was relieved to still have it.

"You could kill a bull with some of this stuff," the Chief said. "What the hell is this?" He held up a kit.

Wendel pointed at the name on the package: "Blind Hole Bearing Puller Set."

"I can read," the Chief said. "What's it for?"

"To pull a bearing out of a blind hole."

"Yeah, right."

"You've taken my computers, how I make a living. Now you're taking half my belongings. I'll have to check into a homeless shelter just to get a meal. Next you'll want my bed."

"You think this is a big joke, Wendel. You're in serious trouble."

"I had nothing to do with killing Gorman. I never liked the guy, but we've been talking." Wendel related how Gorman was offering him money and had helped him print the pictures. "He showed me all his office equipment," Wendel added to be sure the Chief knew there was a legitimate reason for his fingerprints to turn up in Gorman's study.

"Did you see anyone on the beach when you were supposedly swimming?" the Chief asked.

"A yacht buzzed the coast just as I got out. I thought it was a little close, but that's not unusual. I think it was high tide, which would have made it more difficult for someone to walk in the loose sand on the steep slope." Wendel retrieved his tide book from the kitchen and showed it to the Chief. "People can walk through the yards on the other side of the street. Has the guard told you about other people who've driven through this afternoon?"

"I hope you don't have any plans to leave town," the Chief said.

"I don't," Wendel said after mulling over whether overnight in Salinas really constituted leaving town.

"As far as I'm concerned, you're suspect number one."

Wendel was about to say something about being under house arrest but didn't want to tempt the Chief. He stumbled for an answer other than his usual flip comments, which the Chief wasn't appreciating at the moment. The doorbell interrupted his thoughts. The odor-elimination company had come to pick up the ozonator and fans, just when they might be needed at the Gorman's, even though Gorman's body hadn't been lying around for long.

After the Chief and the ozonator departed, Wendel poured the rest of the white Burgundy he had opened for Gorman less than a week ago and sat on the patio. For the first time since finding Handler he was frightened. Margo used to say he lived in denial of unpleasant realities, but he could no longer think that Handler's death was an isolated event that had nothing to do with him. At least someone had killed Gorman and not him. He'd been an available target, exposed in the ocean, doubly exposed in the hot tub. Being a suspect for a murder he hadn't committed stoked his anxiety. Someone could have stolen one of his knives and used it to kill Gorman. Paranoia seeped into his thoughts as he pictured the police finding the knife with his fingerprints on it.

On the way out to dinner he saw that the new guard was the same one he had brought In 'n Out burgers. He stopped and asked if he could bring something from the pub in the village. The guard gave him a thumbs-up and requested a ham sandwich with fries. Wendel was about to drive on but first asked if they kept a log of visitors, and the guard showed him the list. Several deliveries, some women to play bridge at the Strawbridge's, wow. Brendan Wilde's name at 1:00 P.M., with the entry showing that Brendan had come to see Wendel. Brendan was around for both the murders.

Wendel parked in front of the hardware store, walked up the street and was not unduly surprised to find Brendan having a burger at the bar at the pub.

After Wendel ordered a draught and a burger with onions, Brendan said, "I was headed south to visit my mother and stopped to see if you were around." He had learned about Gorman's murder from Myrna when he stopped to say hello to the Chief and see if he had learned anything about Handler's murder.

"You came by my house earlier when I wasn't there." Wendel said, looking for Brendan's reaction.

"I was going to ask about a bed for the night, but when I learned you were the prime suspect, I figured I should stay out of the way, at least for the day."

"You've been here for both murders. Why aren't you a suspect?"

"I probably am, even though I have no motive."

"You're riding all over the country, and the Chief tells me I have to stay in town."

"They can't tell you not to travel unless they arrest you."

"I'm supposed to go to Salinas tomorrow, which I didn't tell him.

" Salinas?"

Wendel related the phone message from Victor Zvolens and their conversation about the Klee.

"What do you know about Zvolens?" Brendan asked.

"Not much. He's into vineyards and art."

"I've heard about a Zvolens who supposedly controls the supply of farm workers, solves immigration problems, maybe shady. I don't know if he's in Salinas."

"Doesn't sound like the kind of guy who'd be interested in modern art."

"You'll find out if you go."

After Wendel finished his beer and bought the ham sandwich and fries for the guard, Brendan followed him home to spend the night, and agreed to drive him to the Anaheim Amtrak station the next morning. Wendel couldn't shake the thought that Brendan's arrival was more than coincidence, and yet he couldn't see him as the killer. He had the ability but no motive, and besides Wendel's intuition kept dismissing the idea.

12

Wendel stuffed a change of clothes, toothbrush and razor into a backpack, rolled the large Klee copy under the backpack's flap and climbed onto Brendan's motorcycle. At the station Brendan said, "Be careful. Handler's murder seemed like a fluke, maybe a burglary gone bad, but two in the neighborhood. You have no idea what's going on."

Wendel considered his friend's warning while riding the commuter train to LA. He had already decided not to be careful by not leaving all this to the police. No way to be careful and still follow what he feared was becoming an obsession to figure out the murders and loss of the painting he had always loved but considered worthless.

On the Coast Starlight headed north, he turned down a private compartment because his creativity thrived in unfamiliar places, and the compartment would be too much like working at home. He carefully stuck the backpack in the rack above the seat, sat down and called the police station. Fortunately the Chief was out so he could leave a message rather than tell him he was leaving town.

Before he got comfortable, a boy about five sat down behind him and struck up a conversation. "Where was Wendel going? Why? How long? Did he have any little boys?" Wendel answered each question, asked his own and finally told the kid he needed to be quiet to do some work.

He tried to focus on security for GeTechNome, traps and triggers for online intruders, and he jotted down a few ideas. He came up with nothing he couldn't circumvent himself, proof of the inadequacy of the idea. The kid's chattering behind him and occasional kick to the back of Wendel's seat forced him to concentrate. A man next to him—after Oxnard the car had no empty double seats—was reading a book entitled, "Achieve Your Leadership Potential," and was highlighting entire pages with his yellow marker.

Wendel took out his phone and called Victor Zvolens to confirm their meeting.

"You're actually taking a train?" Zvolens said.

"It's even on time," Wendel said.

Zvolens asked where he was staying and when Wendel said he planned to walk from the station to the In 'n Out Burger and then find a motel nearby, Zvolens said, "No you're not. My men will pick you up at the station, and you're staying in the guest suite at my vineyard."

Wendel didn't argue. When he got off the phone, the kid was singing, "Down came the rain and washed the spider out." Only he sang the line over and over and over rather than sing the entire ditty, overwhelming all the cell-phone talk going on around him that Wendel had been able to concentrate through.

Unable to think, Wendel turned and said, "Hey kid. How about 'Out came the sun and dried the spider out?'"

The kid replied, "Down came the rain and washed the spider out." The woman with the kid, who wore a tight t-shirt emblazoned with, "teen power," was absorbed into whatever her iPod was pumping into her head. She ignored them both.

"Exercise some of that power," Wendel said to her.

"What?"

"Forget it."

Wendel was pleased with the list of 12 security ideas he carried off the train in his backpack. He wound through the people waiting to board and saw two men down the platform with a hand-drawn sign that said, "Mr. Wendel." One took his pack as they walked toward a black stretch limo in the parking lot. They all climbed into the back where a sack of In 'n Out cheeseburgers and fries awaited them along with a fridge stocked with wine, beer and sodas.

"Mr. Zvolens says you have some pictures to show him," one of the men said as he started into his second burger.

They looked Latino—dark hair Wendel would gladly have accepted in exchange for his own growing forehead, plus earthy skin from a mixture of heritage and sun. Both spoke English without an accent. He guessed they were second generation, probably born shortly before or after their parents arrived from Latin America. Both were dressed in unbleached jeans and both were perfectly mannered, typical of Latinos raised by first generation immigrants.

Wendel pointed to the backpack and said, "In there." He pulled out the rolled copy and spread it for them to see."

"Kind of wild," one said. His iron-pumped body bulged at his t-shirt that he wore without a jacket even though the temperature had plunged at least into the forties.

"Like some of Mr. Z's stuff," said the taller man with a carefully sculpted goatee.

"Mr. Zvolens asked us to bring the painting so he could study it tonight," said Iron-Pumper. Wendel had fallen into a bad habit of forgetting names.

"I'd like to show it to him myself."

"He's tied up till late."

"I've got some work to do until he's free," Wendel said.

"He'd like to have time alone with the painting."

Wendel didn't want to give it up but couldn't think of a good reason not to. He had the flash storage in his pocket with the copy from the email and could print more if necessary. Still Iron-Pumper's last statement sounded more like a command than a request and commands always challenged Wendel. He was in enough trouble from yesterday's challenge of the Chief's Post-It on his front door, so he said, "Sure, he can have it overnight." Might save time in the morning, Wendel figured.

The vineyard suite was the nicest accommodation Wendel had ever landed. Even Margo would be satisfied. King-sized bed with a plush pillow-top on the mattress, restored antique furniture or new stuff chipped and nicked to look antique, a desk "for your work," Goatee said, and another well-stocked fridge, a home entertainment center with a giant screen and a stack of recent-vintage movies plus a cabinet that Goatee unlocked containing a pornography library.

To hell with work, Wendel thought as he inserted a George Clooney movie and poured the rest of the Chardonnay they had opened in the limo. Before getting comfortable he examined the paintings on the wall, all original oils, none of the artists or works familiar to Wendel.

For the first time in his life a rooster woke Wendel, before six. He washed his face and spent an hour considering some of his security code ideas for GeTechNome, gaining confidence he could convince the scientists to give it a try. Zvolens' men came by at 8 as Wendel was stuffing his backpack. Together they walked to a brick colonial building and into a large plush office, leather chairs, dark-wood furniture, and art as dense on the walls as any museum Wendel had visited. Two place settings along with a large pitcher of orange juice sat on a round table, presumably for Wendel and Zvolens.

"We leave you here," Goatee said and held out his hand. When Iron-Pumper gripped Wendel's hand, he didn't let go. Nor could Wendel pull back. Each time he tried, Iron-Pumper's grip tightened.

"A word of caution," Iron-Pumper said. Mr. Zvolens wants you to know that your meeting today is confidential, not to be discussed with anyone." Wendel pulled harder and again Iron-Pumper squeezed harder. Afraid the man would break his hand, Wendel gave up. "I want you to know that we love Mr. Zvolens. Neither of us wants you to disappoint Mr. Z. Not that you've disappointed him, but whatever happens today, we didn't want you to be tempted."

Left alone Wendel shook out his hand. He liked both those guys but wished he were Brendan and could have thrown the son-of-a-bitch onto his ass. Before he could sort through the importance of confidentiality and disappointing Zvolens, a man walked into the room and said, "Good morning, Mr. Wendel. I am Victor Zvolens." He had to be aware of his employees' treatment, yet he seemed so welcoming and congenial that Wendel had a sliver of doubt.

The sore hand didn't prevent Wendel from swallowing the orange juice, omelet, bacon, toast, and coffee served to them by an attractive Latino woman somewhere between 30 and 50—Wendel could never tell. "Let me know if you want anything else," she said to Wendel. You too, Senor Zvolens," she said with a familiarity that made her seem something other than a servant, perhaps Zvolens' woman, though maybe only a natural reaction to the relaxed ambience Zvolens emanated.

"I hope you slept well, Mr. Wendel," Zvolens said. "Call me Victor by the way."

Wendel explained that people called him by his last name. "Forget the mister," he said. "Great apartment. Thanks for having me."

"I always think of Wendel as a kind of...wimpy, shall we say, first name, so I'm pleased you are a last-name-only person."

Zvolens related how his older brother had led him from Hungary to Naples during World War II, making Wendel wonder what this history had to do with the Klee that Zvolens had studied the night before. The brother and Zvolens had sailed together on a boat that the United

States turned away but that took them to Canada. Then after the war they came to California where Zvolens grew up, went to school and worked as a farm laborer, saving his money until he began buying land in what later became valuable grape-growing country. He sounded proudest when he spoke of earning an MBA in vineyard management and hospitality. Wendel nibbled a piece of cold bacon and then some cheese from the omelet, delighted to be the beneficiary of most of Zvolens' hospitality. His right hand again felt the same as the other so why complain.

"I also began collecting art," Zvolens said. He gestured toward the walls, and for the first time Wendel realized all the paintings were modern or contemporary art, including at least two that looked Klee-like. "Yes they are," Zvolens said reading his mind. "Not all that valuable, though."

The woman cleared the table allowing Zvolens to lay out Wendel's Klee. "This is very interesting," Zvolens said. "Tell me the whole story of how you found it and also how you lost it."

Wendel related the three-dollar purchase and then how he found Handler dead and the picture gone. He told Zvolens about the email from Burgher at the Klee Entwurf announcing that the picture not only was a copy, which of course Zvolens knew, but also was a copy of something created by someone other than Klee.

"I agree that Klee wouldn't have had the silkscreen facilities to make this by 1940 when he died," Zvolens said. "What was written on the back of the print?"

"No idea," Wendel said. "I had it framed 25 years ago in St. Louis, Missouri and never looked."

"I guess the frame was stolen also?"

"It wasn't around, though it would have been difficult for someone to cart off, especially on a motorcycle, which is my guess as to who has it." Wendel got up and examined both Klee drawings, neither of which was larger than an 8-1/2 by 11 piece of paper. Both were black and white with a tremendous amount of detail.

"The one on the right is a wash drawing," Zvolens said. "Pencil on the left. Neither of great value, low five figures at most. After all Klee did almost nine thousand drawings and paintings, maybe many more. No one's certain. Why do you think it was a motorcyclist? It wouldn't be easy to carry on a motorcycle."

Wendel explained that he cycled and that riders often dropped by his house for Sunday-morning gospel music. "Bikers had been there about the time Handler had been killed."

"Do you ever get any...radicals, shall we say?" Zvolens asked.

"I get all kinds including some unusual types, but I have no idea if they're radical. If the Klee's aren't worth much, why are you interested in my copy of a fake? Even if Klee painted it, mine is a cheap copy."

"By radical I mean anti-government types."

"How about a survivalist?" Wendel explained how his friend Brendan rode with someone called, "The Hammer," who according to Brendan wanted to be left alone by the government. "I met the man, and I didn't think he was crazy, so I doubt if he thinks he's going to take over the government."

"They want to overthrow, not take over the government. I'll let you in on a secret, Wendel, but first I want to show you my winery." Wendel had taken vineyard tours, and didn't need another narration about processing the grapes, the vats and the casks, bottling, choice of corks, but Zvolens wasn't the type to be dissuaded. Zvolens, who was a couple inches shorter than Wendel, 5' 10" at most, and looked like he had never added a pound to his waist as revealed by his perfectly tailored khakis, led him to a tasting room where the sommelier was breaking out a bottle of last year's pinot noir. She poured a third of the way up in two snifters. Zvolens swirled both with a grace that Wendel had never achieved with his swirls, which often spun over the top of his glass, and then handed one to Wendel.

Wendel tried to look like he knew what he was doing by sticking his nose in the glass, pausing, and then taking a sip. Smooth. Neither heavy nor thin. He liked it and said so.

Zvolens drove them in a golf cart over the dirt roads that separated his vineyard fields, pointing out the different grapes. Harvests would be complete in another couple weeks, and cool nights had already turned many leaves to a mixture of yellow and brown. They approached some older buildings that looked like they were no longer part of the operation. Yet when they stopped Wendel saw they were all reinforced with new lumber and steel supports.

Zvolens removed the padlock from one and then fished out a key that opened the deadbolt. He flipped on a light, revealing a large room full of weapons. After Wendel looked around for a moment, he thought he had entered a quartermaster's shop for the Third Reich. Uniforms with swastikas hung on hangers across the back of the room. Helmets lined a shelf. Hand grenades another. A third shelf held handguns including some Wendel recognized as Lugers from World War II movies. To one side of the room was an assortment of shells and small artillery pieces, a couple bazookas, a rack of rifles like the racks Wendel recalled from the army. A musty odor reflected the age of the items. A nearby warble from a bird felt out of place.

He didn't know what to say, was wary, actually fearful that he was about to get some Nazi thuggery, an escalation of the Iron-Pumper's handshake. Zvolens watched him with an amused expression.

"You're wondering what this is all about. I told you that when I was a child I escaped the Nazis. The Nazis killed my father. My mother fought against them, and after they caught her, they raped her." He concealed all but a trace of emotion that seemed more disgust with the Nazi baseness than anger or feeling for his mother. After the war my brother found her and even though she was only 29 years old when they moved to Canada, she was an old woman who no longer wanted to live. You must know neo-Nazis live in the United States. Wherever I find them, I oppose them. These are the souvenirs I've picked up along the way. The other buildings have all of their modern weapons I've confiscated."

"What's that have to do with radicals?" Wendel asked. "That guy, the Hammer, probably would be on your side against Nazis."

"Hitler succeeded because Europe was unstable. Neo-Nazis will accept help from any de-stabilizing source."

"What if they break in and cart off this stuff?"

"We of course will not let that happen. Now let us go back and look at your painting."

He turned off the light and re-locked the door. On the drive back Wendel wondered if Zvolens was crazy, afraid skinheads and survivalists who hated each other would take over the world. The man acted obsessed. But Wendel also was obsessed with chasing down killers and his painting. Maybe we're both crazy, he thought.

Back in the office they sat again at the table with the copy of the Klee. "I have told you probably more than you want to know. I trust that you will not reveal any of this. I have checked on you, and learned you are a loner, no great friend of the authorities, but not a radical. As you might have guessed, I would like your help." The woman who had served them breakfast set down cups and offered coffee or tea. After the drinks were settled and poured, Zvolens said, "When Klee was born, his parents lived near Bern. Yet he was born a German citizen because his father was German, which is what mattered to the Swiss. He spent most of his life in Germany and taught at the Bauhaus as you undoubtedly know since you are a collector. However the Nazis shut down the Bauhaus, claiming what it taught was un-German, and then in 1933, they condemned Klee for producing degenerate art. Which was why he moved back to Switzerland."

Zvolens pulled the painting closer. "I've always been drawn by Herr Klee's almost childlike art." He traced the legs of the stick figure that looked to Wendel like the man was jumping a hurdle. Wendel also had been drawn to this print because of Klee's childlike quality. "My happiest days were when I was a child," Zvolens said, "when I lived in Hungary with my mother and father." He paused and sat for a moment as though revisiting and re-experiencing this most happy time, lost to him because of the war. Wendel wondered what it was like to have his happiest times behind him before growing up. The lines in Zvolens's face told Wendel that childlike memories had been subsumed by the complex burdens of adult life, much more complex than the sheltered existence Wendel tried to maintain.

Zvolens continued: "Mr. Burgher at the Klee Entwurf probably figured this was a copy of a silkscreen because of these feathery lines, typical of silkscreen prints. Also the signature is too large for Klee who was quite modest in signing his art, usually an insignificant 'Klee' at the bottom. So I can see why he didn't think this was done by Klee.

"However, Klee sometimes painted with watercolors which also produce feather-like strokes, leaving negative space, paper with no paint. Some people believe that Klee painted several large watercolors late in his life, larger than most of his work, maybe more the size of your so-called 'print.' The story goes that he painted a small series of anti-Nazi art. Look at yours. Perhaps all this blind passion in a man in a hurry is meant to describe the German people, so quick to blindly follow Hitler. What do you think?"

Zvolens paused while Wendel considered the interpretation, which could easily fit. He said, "I'm trying to recall the painting I bought. Could it have been a watercolor?" He had liked it immediately, then argued with Margo who at first complained but then said, "So what— for three dollars we'll hide it in your office." Yet he hadn't studied the painting. The man at the store had rolled it up, slipped a rubber band around it and handed it to him. Back home before having it framed, he showed it to some friends, his brother and his father, none of whom had been particularly interested. They didn't know any more about Klee than he did. "I have no idea if it's a watercolor. I don't know much about art, and back then knew even less."

"None of these paintings in the so-called series have turned up," Zvolens said. "Yours would be the first. People who believe Klee painted these watercolors believe the Nazis made a special effort to confiscate them, even sending spies to Switzerland during the war. Still some may have survived, and perhaps a soldier brought yours to the United States."

"If someone went to that trouble he wouldn't be selling it for three dollars," Wendel said.

"Soldiers collect souvenirs and then get tired of them. Klee wasn't a household name back—"

Wendel's phone interrupted them. He hated to interrupt Zvolens but didn't want to cross the Chief more than he already had. He apologized and then answered.

"How long will it take you to get back here," the Chief said.

"This evening if I catch the afternoon train. What's the rush?" He turned on the speakerphone so that Zvolens would know he had no choice but to cut short their meeting.

"The FBI has analyzed your computers. You have some explaining to do. I'm tempted to send a man up to bring you back."

After he promised to be there and explained that he could have ignored the call if he didn't want to cooperate, and even offered to come in as soon as his train arrived around eleven, the Chief agreed to meet him at eight the next morning at the police station.

13

"You have to leave," Zvolens said. "No rush. I will fly you to the Long Beach Airport."

"Sounds good to me," Wendel said, ignoring his thought, really question, of how much experience Zvolens had flying. He must have some experience, and since Wendel had never flown in a private plane, he wanted to give it a try.

"Good," Zvolens said. "We have time to clarify a few things."

Here comes, Wendel thought.

"I want your Klee painting. Of course I will pay you a reasonable price. You can continue to hang this copy which is what you've always supposed you had."

"That might work," Wendel said. "Only I don't have the Klee. I'm here because I thought you could help me find it."

"I can, with your assistance. I would wager that neo-Nazis working with the radicals took your painting. They know me and won't deal with me. They now even know my men when I send them. I need you to bird dog the painting."

"Sniff out or snuff out," Wendel said. He told Zvolens about Gorman's death and how he had become a suspect.

"From what you say about Mr. Gorman, I wouldn't be surprised if he was one of them. I can investigate that, and I understand you are a computer expert so maybe you can also."

"And he collects art. Maybe he had the Klee and they came for it. It has become a popular piece of art."

"Because of your mister Handler."

"Look, Victor. I'm crazy enough to mix with those guys, something I plan to do on a motorcycle trip to Idaho week after next. I'll be with a survivalist but he's no Nazi."

"Still you might find something."

"I'll look around. But I can't take them on. How about if I mix in and if necessary you mix it up."

"That's what I have in mind. You find that painting, I'll retrieve it. And if you find an arsenal, I will take care of that too."

With their understanding in hand, Zvolens deferred to one of his pilots to shuttle Wendel on what turned out to be a Hawker 1000, a jet Wendel had never heard of but could easily work into his travel schedule. He moved from soft leathery seat to soft leathery seat, enjoying the cush and straining to hear if the engines made even the slightest noise. The 30-minute flight gave him only enough time to realize how far he was in over his head. Brendan could give him cover to play with the survivalists or Nazi bikers or whatever they were, but mountain biking was a lot different from rummaging through some group's headquarters for a painting that was sure to be hidden. He didn't have much choice—Zvolens had more directed than asked him. Besides he looked forward to the trip, exhilarated by the mystery and the possibility of danger. He could always exaggerate his search and tell Zvolens he didn't find anything. And as Zvolens said, he'd always have the copy to hang on his wall. He landed in Long Beach in time to see the Chief that afternoon, but instead went home and prepared his Monday presentation to the GeTechNome scientists.

Next morning in the Chief's office Wendel was half awake when the Chief greeted him in a gnarly mood, complaining that Wendel was taking too much of his time. The Chief fumbled around his messy desk as if looking for proof that Wendel had committed the crime of becoming "high maintenance."

"How about we talk over at Starbucks?" Wendel said. "I'll buy."

"We can add attempted bribery to the charges," the Chief said.

Wendel rolled his eyes and after pleading, the Chief let him fetch for each of them. "Mediums," Wendel said at the counter refusing to accept the Starbucks lingo even though he was hooked on their coffee.

"The Feds say you forwarded the date on your computer two days," the Chief said reading from what was likely an FBI report. "They think you meant to set it back two days so it would look like you were still in Europe when you received certain emails."

"They're wrong," Wendel snapped, offended that someone would question his computer competence. "I meant to set it two days forward so I could set it back before turning it over to you. That way if something turned up it would look like I gave it to you as soon as I became aware of it."

"I don't get it," the Chief said.

"You grabbed my other computer the night I got home, and I needed a computer to do some work. I told you the other day I could get you Handler's emails faster than the Feds could."

The Chief eyed him as though not sure of what to make of Wendel's admission of deception. Wendel was following Brendan's advice to keep a lie as close to the truth as possible, and in fact what he was saying wasn't even a lie, just incomplete. And if the Chief wanted to know what he found on the computer, he'd tell him.

"Turns out your painting is more important than I thought," the Chief said.

"I always knew it was important."

"Handler emailed some guy in Switzerland about the painting. The Swiss guy didn't reply. End of story except I had the Feds check with the airlines and this Swiss guy, Burgher, flies into LAX and then out the next day. We check some more and learn Burgher called Handler's gallery to find out where he was staying and what he was doing in the U.S."

Wendel was hardly listening at first, wondering why the email back he had discovered by hacking onto Burgher's computer wasn't found on his own computer. Sloppy feds, a thought he kind of liked. Then when the Chief said that Burgher had flown to LA, Wendel not only started paying more attention, wondering what he might have missed, but also gained respect for the Chief's detective abilities.

"He flew here from Lucerne?"

"That's what I said."

"Why haven't you had the guy arrested? It sounds like he flew here, killed Handler, grabbed the painting and flew home."

"I wish it were that simple," the Chief said. "Trouble is he flew back to Switzerland two days before the earliest possible date of death for Handler."

"So he had someone else kill Handler," Wendel said.

"He came here with a five million dollar international letter of credit, which he cancelled two days later without using it. Maybe he had Handler killed because Handler wouldn't sell him the painting."

Wendel sat back. He had hardly touched his coffee, now lukewarm, though even cold coffee might help him understand what the Chief was up to. "So why are you telling me all this?" he asked. "Yesterday you were ready to send a posse after me."

"I thought you'd want to follow up on the painting. We don't have the money to traipse over to Switzerland without more evidence, but you might be interested."

Wendel held back a laugh at the idea of both Zvolens and the Chief deputizing him, like some gunslinger out of the old west. Only Wendel would have a better chance of slinging a gun across the room than trying to shoot the thing.

"Handler probably told Burgher he didn't own the painting, that I owned it," Wendel said. "Isn't it likely Burgher hired someone to kill Handler and steal the painting?"

"A hunch," the Chief said. "But not enough to arrest him. Maybe if we get something more. That's why we don't mind getting your help."

"But you think I killed Gorman."

"Just because you're my number one suspect, doesn't mean I'm ready to arrest you. If you disappear in Switzerland or Rio, we'll chase you down."

"I'm free to go?"

"You are. By the way if you're such a computer hotshot, you probably know that Handler searched through your documents sometime the day he died."

How did I miss that Wendel thought on the way out? He hadn't had much time before the Chief took his computer, and fortunately he didn't have much to hide—a meager bank account and a more meager "black book." Handler was kind of nosy, but Wendel couldn't be too critical having gone through Handler's desk during the house swap.

Late that afternoon Wendel sat in the hot tub with Cheryl, sipping a glass of Bryant Cabernet, which Cheryl informed him sold for a thousand dollars a bottle. He didn't even like Cabernets, but couldn't resist the extravagance.

"There's a guy in Switzerland who thinks the Klee's a valuable watercolor," he told Cheryl. "A guy in Salinas who thinks the same and believes some radicals from Idaho, who happened to drop by my house, stole it. Maybe the guy in Switzerland's a Nazi. I can probably live with just a copy, but I can't get this business out of my mind. Which is just as good because the guy in Salinas might off me if I don't chase down this painting."

"Maybe the painting and the murders aren't connected," Cheryl said.

"I had that thought when I met Margo on Monday," Wendel said and told Cheryl about how she had spent an afternoon with Handler and then maybe needed to silence him.

"She's one tough chick," Cheryl said. "She calls me for lunch now and then, I think just to check up on you, be sure you're not prospering too much."

"She hated the painting but if Handler told her it was valuable, she might have taken it."

"The murder doesn't have to be connected with the painting," Cheryl said.

"Why do you keep saying that?"

"My husband used to call it thinking outside the package," she said.

"Outside the box. Package was what your husband didn't give you enough of."

"Speaking of that," she said, "I met a guy up at Esalen who could give me plenty of packages. At the moment though I'm a little short. Any chance you could make me a loan?"

Wendel had recently increased the loan on his house and was flush for the moment, but not for long if GeTech-Nome didn't pay him or Margo's husband didn't come through with some work. "How much do you need?"

"Ten thousand."

"Like to cover a trip to Trader Joe's," he said.

"I could struggle with five but I need to find ten somewhere to invite this guy down from Fresno and show him a decent time."

"Fresno and Esalen don't sound like a mix," he said.

"Charley didn't realize that the Deepak-Chopra-type workshop on how to increase your wealth wasn't about investments until he got there. Which was great because he wasn't interested in the new-age platitudes and had plenty of time for me."

"I won't ask the details, but what happens if he doesn't come through?"

"I'll get your money back for you." She didn't hide her irritation with what to her must have sounded like reluctance."

"I'm more worried about you than my money."

"What will happen? I'll have to sell my house. Gorman had friends who wanted to live in the neighborhood. They probably still do."

Wendel looked around the yard, couldn't imagine some Gormanite as his next-door neighbor, who would probably get rid of the bird feeders, tear out the overgrown bush and build a formal garden. He reached over the side of the tub and pulled a phone out of the pocket of his robe, searching back several calls to find a number.

"You're going to electrocute us," Cheryl said.

"Just a gentle shock with this battery," he said. "Can I speak to Mr. Zvolens? This is Wendel."

After a moment the operator said, "We're looking for him, Mr. Wendel."

"I'll get you the money," he said to Cheryl. "Maybe I can save a few bucks with this call."

"So soon, Wendel," said Zvolens.

Wendel told him what the Chief had passed on about Burgher flying over from Lucerne, and then added, "Can that plane of yours fly to Switzerland. I think I should go and don't have the cash."

"Yes you must go to Lucerne. I will fly with you and spend a few days in Hungary."

"Mind if I bring a pretty woman."

"Wouldn't mind at all. She'll add cover. You're a man with his girlfriend trying to find out something about his painting."

They agreed on the next Tuesday, the day after his presentation to the GeTechNome scientists. Wendel would call Burgher, tell him that he was the owner of the fake Klee, that he'd always valued it and still did even though it was a fake, and that he wanted to learn more about Klee. He wouldn't tell Burgher that he knew it was an original watercolor, at least not over the phone.

"Who's your girl?" Cheryl said after he hung up.

"You. Could be a fun trip."

"You rascal. Do I have to go to get the money?"

"The money's yours whether you go or not. This guy Zvolens is rich so maybe the trip's a two-for."

"Can't I go as your wife?"

"We can manage that, but before you agree, you should know the trip could be dangerous. Maybe this guy hired someone to kill Handler."

"Not likely if he brought the money to buy the painting."

"Unless the money wasn't enough once he saw it."

Wendel took an extra glance at Cheryl as she wrapped herself into her robe and decided he liked the husband-wife scenario. At home he was exhilarated with his growing adventure. His casual decision to opt for danger felt like a child's reckless disregard of consequences or even a drunk's reeling through the streets after the bars closed. He liked the feeling. His search for Handler's killer gave adventure to his life beyond his usual games, which was how he characterized solving his clients' technology challenges. Even GeTechNome made him feel more alive, probably because of the risk of losing his fee if he couldn't make the scientists comfortable.

He packed some clothes and sat down to figure where to take a three-day bike trip to celebrate his high spirits. Easier to plan Monday's presentation while alone in the hills. And he liked going to Europe as husband and wife with Cheryl. The thought of losing her to some fat cat made him realize how much he liked her.

14

Sally Simms met Wendel at the GeTechNome security station and led him to Frances Holmes' office. Frances had done some early work deciphering the human genome before leaving to start her biotech business. Each year she was recommended for a Nobel Prize for biology and the past two years, her company liked to let people know, she had been recommended for two prizes, the second being the Peace Prize for using her wealth and influence as catalysts for improving health care in undeveloped countries. She also collected art, which she hung on the company's walls, including, Wendel noticed, two Klees outside her office. Wendel recognized one from a photo in a Klee book Zvolens kept in his guest suite.

"Your project is vitally important," she told Wendel as they settled at a table. Large companies can save energy, and this plan will be a model for others." She had no desk in her office, only three round, oak card tables. "When the meeting starts, I'll introduce you." Not that Wendel needed an intro—he had interviewed each of the scientists to learn their needs and concerns. "I'm afraid," she continued, "some of my scientists, led by Waldo Peterson, are undermining the program."

"He's a bit of a Luddite," Sally said.

"He's a contrarian," Wendel said. "If I said I think GeTechNome is the greatest bio-tech company in the world, he'd want to fight about it."

"That's what makes him a great scientist," Frances said. "Like Albert Einstein, he challenges any conventional idea. The others like him so you can't marginalize him. I want to be certain you're ready to deal with him."

Wendel resisted the urge to shrug, his natural reaction because who could ever say they were ready for a Peterson. Instead he said he was prepared and told them he had studied and developed a sound security system. A friend at SRI, the Stanford research center that had developed significant computer security systems, had confirmed and blessed his approach. He did not tell them he hadn't prepared a pitch for today's meeting because he fell flat delivering a planned speech. He liked to wing it.

Frances stood up, as did Wendel and Simms. "You like Paul Klee," he said as they walked out of the office.

"They're among my favorites."

"Are you aware of a series of anti-Nazi watercolors Klee painted in 1939 or 40?"

She paused to look at Wendel as if wondering what Klee's watercolors might have to do with anything important, or perhaps wondering how a guy she probably saw as a geek knew anything about art. "I'm not. What about them?"

Wendel didn't want to take her time with the whole story about the Klee and the murder, so he said, "A collector told me about them. If it's true, what do you think one would be worth today?"

"Twenty-five or thirty million dollars," she said with a chuckle. "If you have one, let me know."

As he waited to be introduced, Wendel tried to get his mind off how rich he'd be if he found his painting, realizing he better decide on what he would say to the scientists. Waldo Peterson sat at the far left side at the front of the room, a kind of lecture or presentation room with rows of tables and chairs. Wendel would have preferred a round-table setup, better for dialogue than a lecture. The room with no windows or art radiated a chill. Frances explained how important the project was, though not as important as the scientists in the room whom she encouraged to become comfortable.

Wendel explained that each scientist would carry a keychain device programmed to pick up a password that would change on the device every ten seconds. Within the ten seconds the scientist would have to key the password into a home laptop to enter the GeTechNome system. Because the passwords become invalid after ten seconds, hackers cannot retrieve and use them.

"Any system can be cracked," Peterson interjected. He leaned back in his chair cracking sunflower seed shells with his teeth as if to emphasize his point. He swallowed the seeds and spit the shells into a coffee cup he had brought to the meeting.

"I agree," Wendel said. He walked around the dais and sat on the table next to it. "Just like any building can be broken into. So I've developed some backup security to deal with a successful intruder, just like I'm sure you have systems to catch someone who manages to break in here."

"How do we deal with intruders?" one of the scientists said.

"We keep that a secret," Frances said.

"You probably have sophisticated systems like motion detectors," Wendel said, knowing full well, having talked with security, that they did not have the detectors.

"We are the motion detectors," Peterson said. "There's always someone here nights and weekends, often several of us."

"I'd hate to be the early warning system," said one of the scientists.

Wendel couldn't tell if Frances was pleased or pissed with the anxiety he'd raised as a straw man to make his point that no security system was one hundred percent safe. Regardless he welcomed the somewhat chaotic discussion, which fit his style and blurred the focus on his system.

As he explained the backup for his codes if they were broken, Frances got up and left the room. Not only would the scientists have to electronically "sign in," but that they could set up their experiments to shut down if they received a direction outside expected parameters. He inserted a flash storage into the room's computer and ran several Power Point shots to illustrate. They didn't add much but scientists and business people worshipped Power Point.

"What keeps a hacker from changing those parameters?" Peterson said.

"Each of you would have to enter a code before a change could be made, and yes, a sophisticated computer person could crack those codes as well," Wendel said. "But right now, if a destructive person is working at three A.M. and is the only person here, what keeps him from lousing up someone else's experiment? What I'm trying to get across is that while I can provide heavy security, nothing is foolproof with any system, and electronics can be more secure than buildings."

While he was talking Frances returned, and when he finished, she said, "I just checked and we never considered having motion detectors. With people working all kinds of hours, they're a problem. We haven't dealt with security for several years so I'm going to hire a consultant to see that we have the latest and best."

"They'll probably put in cameras to spy on us," Peterson said. "You won't be able to take a leak in private." He drew some laughs. The guy was outrageous, but Wendel, reminded of some of his own antics, kind of liked him.

"Things aren't like that around here, Waldo," one of the scientists said.

"I appreciate your skepticism, Waldo," Wendel said. "You've provoked and inspired me to improve what I'm proposing. The doubts of the Waldo Petersons of the world make a company better, and it's probably a pretty good attitude for doing science.

"Here's what I'd like to do," he said. He proposed that in the coming week they each come up with a meaningless experiment as a trial. This would allow them to see how the system would work as well as flush out some of the bugs. He'd work with their IT department to merge his security system into the computer programs. If they felt comfortable with these tests, then some of them could consider putting their experiments, or a part of their experiments at first, on the system. "I suspect there's no way this can work other than voluntarily," he said and noticed several of the scientists shift in their chairs as though relieved. He added that working with advanced computer systems could become a useful skill.

"Plus the advantage of sleeping in every morning," someone said.

"And saving gasoline," another said.

As the scientists packed up their notes and wandered off in twos and threes, Peterson lagged behind. "Got a minute?" he said. Peterson suggested lunch, and they headed for the parking lot, agreeing that Wendel would follow Peterson who had a favorite place in Newport Beach. As Peterson pulled ahead of him, Wendel was shocked to see he drove the old Corvair, the car that had followed him the other day. He tried but couldn't connect Peterson to either Handler or the Klee.

They parked and walked into an Irish pub on the waterfront where the bartender and several of the waiters recognized the scientist. Settled at their table, Peterson said, "I'm not such a bad guy, am I." His smile and tone of voice said he wasn't looking for an answer.

"You've kept me on my toes," Wendel stumbled to say and realized he was shaken by the Corvair.

"You were prepared," Peterson said. "I'll grant you that."

"Thank you, Waldo."

"I could have played dirty. Make a big deal about that murder I read about at your house."

The subject startled Wendel. "What's that have to do with anything?" he said. "I was out of town at the time."

Just then a waitress with a green apron and a shamrock, probably fake, in her hair set a martini on the rocks loaded with cocktail onions in front of Peterson, and took their orders. When she walked off, Wendel was tense and said, "What about the murder?"

"People could get concerned about dealing with you until they catch whoever did it."

"They kill my friend, steal my art and you're concerned about me?"

"Hey take it easy. I didn't mean to stir it up. I'm just up tight about industrial espionage and worry about security." Peterson twiddled his key chain that had a small pillbox attached. He opened the box, removed a single sunflower seed and popped it into his mouth. "Trying to quit smoking," he said. "Terrible, a scientist still smoking."

Wendel struggled to calm down. He didn't want to jump all over Peterson, but hadn't realized how much feeling he was carrying. The Chief suspected him for Gorman's murder, and he was about to fly to Lucerne with Zvolens, who obviously could play rough, not to mention the possibility that Burgher wouldn't be so friendly.

"Maybe I've been working too hard," Wendel said as the waitress delivered his pastrami and Swiss and Peterson's Caesar salad. "Sorry about that. I know it's tough to stop smoking. I used to do it five times a day."

"No problem," Peterson said. "I wanted to talk because I'd like to accommodate Frances whom I adore. I want to get comfortable with these codes and entry systems."

Wendel spread some Dijon mustard onto his pastrami, relieved that his biggest adversary was leaning in the right direction. He seldom worried about money because he'd been able to borrow more and more on his home, but if the bank stopped cooperating.... He needed the GeTechNome fee as well as the prestige and references a successful installation would bring. But a flicker of concern also struck him. Maybe Peterson wanted to learn more so he could attack the system more effectively. And had Peterson been following him?

He gave Peterson some web sites to check plus the name of his friend at SRI. "GeTechNome could even hire SRI to second guess what I've done."

"I can work with you on this. It's got me intrigued, though what happens if someone steals my keychain password device?"

"You call in and cancel communication to your device."

"There'd be a period of vulnerability," Peterson said.

"Yes. There would be." They sat quietly for a few minutes, Peterson apparently unable to add to his concerns, and Wendel waiting to see if having listened to the scientist had alleviated any of his concerns.

"I was thinking by the way," Wendel said, "that you might enjoy coming to one of my church sessions on Sunday mornings at my house. We serve up gospel music along with brunch, Champagne, and an eclectic membership. Lots of motorcycle people. Lots of doubters like yourself." If somehow Peterson were involved with Handler and the Klee, Wendel could see how he reacted back at the scene of the crime.

The offer pleased Peterson who gave Wendel a card so Wendel could email him as to when the next "service" would be.

15

On the tarmac in Long Beach a tanker truck was connecting to Zvolens' jet as Wendel and Cheryl rolled out their bags, which the pilot hoisted up the stairway. A warm Santa Ana breeze wafted unpleasant fumes their way.

"How far does this baby fly?" Wendel asked.

"Plenty," Zvolens said. "Over 3500 miles, which takes us easily from Gander to Europe. From here to Gander is tight, so we'll stop to refuel."

"How tight?" Cheryl said. "A little risk turns me on."

"Lucerne and Herr Burgher will give you enough excitement," Zvolens said. "When it comes to flying, I learned a lesson from my Jewish friends growing up in Hungary. Build a fence around the Torah. If sundown's at six, get home by 5:30."

"Fascinating," Cheryl said. "Are you Jewish? I'd like to hear about growing up in Hungary."

"First we'll get this baby, as Wendel likes to call it, into the air," Zvolens said and disappeared into the cockpit, as Wendel and Cheryl settled into the cush but firm seats.

"Gee whiz, Cheryl," Wendel said. "Next you'll want to sit in his lap and fly the plane."

"He's a good looking guy with money."

"And dangerous."

"I'm surprised you're worried about me. That's sweet."

Too sweet, he thought. Maybe she ought to borrow her ten thousand bucks from Zvolens. Instead he said, "You're supposed to be my wife on this trip. I'm looking out for you. Fasten your belt."

They rose over the ocean and seemed to fly straight up like the Hawker's namesake stalking a prey. Wendel wondered what a "partnership" with Cheryl would be like. At times she was a flake with the different men she entertained, though he wouldn't consider a man a flake for dating different women even if they ended up in bed.

"I get the idea," he said, "that you're not ready to be a wife."

"What do you care?" she said.

"I'd hate to lose a good friend, a good neighbor, someone to share my bomb shelter with."

"Is that all?"

"Maybe more, but I don't have the money you're looking for."

"According to that woman who runs the bio-tech company, if you find your painting, you'll have more money than you can use."

"Sounds like you'd put me in play if I'm rich."

She started to answer, but Zvolens returned. He opened a bottle of Pinot Noir and poured a glass for each of Cheryl and Wendel. As Wendel swirled and inhaled a modest aroma, Zvolens said, "Give it ten minutes to breathe." He was flying co-pilot and said he wouldn't be drinking.

Cheryl told Zvolens about her own Pinots that she kept in Wendel's bomb shelter. Zvolens complimented her taste, and she said the person to compliment was her son-of-a-bitch ex-husband.

"Not too clever a guy to lose you," Zvolens said. "I'd like to try some of those."

"They go down well in my hot tub."

"I'm not surprised as long as you're there."

"Maybe I ought to go up and help fly the plane," Wendel said. "Leave the two of you to talk about Hungary, wine and hot-tubbing."

"The jealous husband," Cheryl said.

Wendel especially resented Zvolens's glibness, which he could never pull off with a woman. Eastern European blood undoubtedly. He couldn't figure out Zvolens who obviously was into dubious activities but acted like Cary Grant in "Roman Holiday" or was it Gary Cooper, or whoever. Really Zvolens was more like Al Pacino in Godfather II who left the rough stuff to people like Zvolens's Iron Pumper and Goatee, which reminded him to ask, "Victor, how about sending your two guys with me when I bike up to Idaho? Assuming we don't find the Klee in Switzerland."

"They're not bikers and if the Hammer is who we think he is, he'd recognize my men."

"I don't think you should go to Idaho," Cheryl said. "That painting's not worth it even if it's an original. You can't enjoy it dead."

Wendel felt a little better that Cheryl was concerned about him. "What do you think, Victor?" he said.

"Mr. Wendel has kindly agreed to be my emissary in these dealings," Zvolens said.

"You want the painting, you should go," Cheryl said.

"Before I go up front to keep Mac awake, I have some suggestions for your meeting with Herr Burgher, whom I've tried to investigate. He has a reputation as a shrewd art dealer and is thought to be involved in other activities about which not much is known. He will probably know more about you, Wendel, than you know about yourself, so you should play it straight. Tell him why you're there, what you know, that you don't think he has the painting, but you're looking for information. This puts more pressure on him. He doesn't know if you know more. Get a feel between the two of you if he is telling the truth."

"He might have the painting," Wendel said.

"Yes, but he returned to Switzerland with his five million so if he does, he's not likely to come out and tell you, even if he didn't kill your friend."

They discussed the pros and cons. The Pinot Noir had blossomed and played with his taste buds, mellowing Wendel's mood. He tended to agree with Zvolens though his thoughts wandered as he looked down on the Great Salt Lake and the mountains around it. He wondered if they could ski in Switzerland in mid September. His conscience nagged at him for not taking their business more seriously as though he didn't value his life. He had even considered breaking into GeTechNome to prove his point that no security system was perfect and certainly would have landed in jail or even been shot by the police.

"If you think Mr. Burgher has the painting," Zvolens continued, "I will have some friends pay him a visit. I doubt if he'll come right out and return it to you. No rush however. Maybe it's in Idaho."

Zvolens excused himself to help fly the plane, and Wendel and Cheryl talked about strategy, agreeing with Zvolens that it was best to tell Burgher the truth.

"Do you trust him," Wendel said nodding toward Zvolens and the cockpit.

"I trust him to do what's best for Zvolens," Cheryl said. "I get the feeling he won't go out of his way to hurt you because he likes you, but he might sacrifice you for the painting."

"If he gets his hands on the Klee, I'll never see him again."

"If we're going to tell Burgher the truth, honey," Cheryl said, exaggerating the "honey," "how can we go as husband and wife?"

"I've been meaning to bring that up," Wendel said. "You've been so preoccupied with your men and now Esalen, it's hard to find a chance."

"Is this a proposal?" she said.

"These days marriage comes last, when the children go off to college."

"Sex comes first," she said. "We've already screwed it up by becoming friends."

"We could remedy that," he said.

"No longer be friends?"

"Is all this talk what they mean by oral sex?" he said.

"More like foreplay," she said. "How about a game of cards before we get carried away only to have your friend, Zvolens, returns with more advice."

In a cabinet behind a Scrabble game, Wendel found a chess set, which reminded him of an erotic chess game from some movie long ago. Cheryl was right. Their conversation had aroused him, even when he thought he was too old for words alone to do the trick. Besides she was fun. What more could he want? She played chess but not very well so that he had to hold back to avoid being excessively dominant before mating her.

They stayed on board in Toronto, but got off and wandered around a mostly desolate Gander airport. Local time was after midnight and the only other flight being serviced was a military transport ferrying United States Army Rangers overseas. From his time in Viet Nam, Wendel remembered the Rangers as a highly trained, gung ho group of warriors, not unlike his friend Brendan, the former Navy Seal. Only once had Wendel stumbled over combat while delivering supplies to troops in the field and felt like a wimp compared to the Rangers. Maybe he was fooling around with Zvolens and survivalists to change his self-image. He only wished he had some Ranger skills.

They listened to Cheryl's iPod that hooked into Zvolens' sound system, avoided more talk of oral sex, and unsuccessfully tried to nap. Cheryl pulled out the latest Oprah magazine and a copy of Anna Karenina and gave Wendel the magazine. He tried to reconcile his "flake" impression of Cheryl with her reading Tolstoy. Maybe he was the flake, the guy looking at pictures of Oprah, so he tossed the magazine aside and took out pencil and notebook to review the software he would install for GeTech-Nome.

At the Zurich airport they caught a train for the half-hour ride to Lucerne. The cool late-summer weather inspired them to walk instead of drive to the Hotel Schweizerhof where Cheryl grasped his arm while he registered. In the room upstairs she said, "Twin beds. How disappointing."

"We can conserve and use only one," Wendel said.

"Keep us warm," she said. "The sign in the lobby said it's getting down to 5 above tonight."

"Centigrade, but still low forties for us."

"If we hop in now, I'll sleep until eight and then be up all night," she said.

They went for a walk, rented a pedal boat and froze their buns in the wind on the lake, joined a crowd in a beer hall where they found a table by the fire, and eventually enjoyed sauerkraut and sausage for dinner. By the time they walked back to the hotel, Wendel wasn't sure if he had the energy to brush his teeth, much less make love. The bed had no top sheet, only a comforter ensconced in a linen wrap, but this strange arrangement wouldn't keep him awake.

"We could do it," he said, "but it wouldn't be memorable, and I'm afraid you might never want to do it again."

"Tomorrow," she said.

16

But the morning found them both keyed up for business. After breakfast they took a cab to Der Klee Entwurf where Burgher's assistant, Elida Wurtz, gave them a tour through scores of Klee paintings and drawings. Wendel eased his necktie's knot, uncomfortable with a grip he had experienced maybe three times, all funerals, since he left IBM.

"Klee certainly had an imagination," Cheryl said.

"That's why he's so loved," Elida said.

"His pictures tell a story," Wendel said.

"Even this pattern?" Cheryl asked. "It looks like my mother's favorite quilt."

"But look at how the cubes tilt this way and that, like a boy's blocks about to fall over," Wendel said.

"Carl Jung would tell you to put yourself into the story rather than try to interpret it," Elida said. "Come, Mr. Burgher should be finished with his meeting."

As they walked through the office corridors Wendel tried to put himself into the story of the toppling blocks. He was starting to feel like his own life might collapse, if Zvolens decided he wasn't doing enough, if the Hammer took a dislike to him in Idaho, under his home mortgage if GeTechNome didn't go ahead with his project.

Jacob Burgher was a hearty man with a significant paunch, a ready smile, and red cheeks that made Wendel wonder if he used rouge. He did not look sinister, nor did his bright orderly office with a talcum-powder aroma. Wendel reminded himself that looks meant nothing, as for example with Zvolens, the rake. Regardless how Burgher turned out, his persona made Wendel comfortable telling his story.

"Shocking," Burgher said when Wendel related how he had found Handler. "I knew of the murder through our police who had inquiries from your police." Without disclosing that he had met Handler in California, Burgher said that Handler was a well-known dealer with whom he had dealt years before.

Wendel said, "I know that Mr. Handler emailed you a picture of the Klee and that you thought the painting was a fake. I knew it was a worthless copy, but I thought it was a copy of a real Klee. What made you think it wasn't?"

Burgher stared at Wendel as though evaluating what he knew and how he knew it. After a moment he scrolled through his computer, found the picture and turned the screen to give them a better look. He laid out the same reasons Zvolens had previously given. "I thought it very clever," Burgher went on. "For example,...," he paused and worked the computer to produce a different painting. "The head is similar to the head in this 1930 Klee, 'Error on Green,' which is in the Galerie Beyeler in Basel. 'Senecio' in Basel's Kunstmuseum has a similar head. 'Flowery Myth' from a private collection has similar color." He showed the pictures as he spoke. "And 'Drummer" from the Klee Foundation in Bern has similar dark lines and whimsical images. But your painting struck me as too symbolic. Klee painted images from his imagination, not deliberate symbols or allegories."

"Maybe by the end of his life after being forced to leave Germany his imagination became more symbolic," Wendel said.

"Most unlikely," Burgher said.

"How much might it be worth if it were a Klee?" Wendel said.

"Yours is a copy so not much. Maybe two hundred of your dollars."

"A collector told me that a watercolor would have some of the same qualities as a silkscreen, the feather appearance in the lines," Wendel said. "Any chance it could be a watercolor."

"You tell me. It's your painting."

Cheryl saved Wendel from admitting he had never looked that closely by asking, "What would an original Klee watercolor be worth?"

"Millions, my dear."

"But not to a thief," she said. "What would a thief do with it? Are there fences like with stolen jewelry?"

"Oh yes. There is a black market. Paintings have been stolen and have never turned up, which makes sense because even innocent buyers are legally required to return stolen paintings. We are certain that some people have large secret collections. You can imagine a well to do person with a vault or a secret room in his mansion."

"It appears someone thought it was real enough to steal it and to kill my friend," Wendel said. "If we enter the underground process between thief and collector, we might find not only the painting but Handler's killer. Any ideas?"

"Too many ideas," Burgher said. "Stay out of that market."

"But if we wanted to pursue it?"

"Do you know the story of Persephone and Hades?"

"Not really," Wendel said.

"I'll spare you the details, but Persephone learned that once you go to the underworld, you cannot readily return. Persephone's mother retrieved her, but I don't think you would be so fortunate."

This sounded like a threat though Burgher's manner and voice hadn't changed. In fact he laughed as though looking for a fence were a joke. Still Burgher must have thought it was an original to have traveled six thousand miles. Wendel doubted if Burgher was trying to be helpful. He obviously was at ease in the close-knit art world in which he probably had countless contacts, not only the museums and legitimate collectors, but also the people who might facilitate a trip to the underworld. Wendel decided to push a little.

"The police wanted us to ask what you learned when you visited Handler in Los Angeles."

"What?" Burgher said, his smile gone.

"The police told us you flew to Los Angeles and back. They might know more they didn't tell us, but they would like to know if you met with Handler and what occurred."

The sun had crept around a building next door so that it shined into Burgher's window onto all three of them, but not so directly that Wendel failed to observe

Burgher's discomfort. He quickly recovered his inscrutability.

"I'm just the messenger of this news," Wendel said, "plus the guy who's looking for his painting. I'm not accusing you."

"And I am trying to help you," Burgher said.

"And I am trying to help you," Wendel said. "The police believe you might be one of the last people to see Handler alive, which is probably what arouses their curiosity."

"Police without curiosity are not really police," Burgher said.

"The police also said that you returned to Switzerland while Handler was still alive which probably means you are not a suspect. I'm sure if you were, they would be asking these questions."

Burgher could not hide his surprise. He stared at Wendel for what seemed like minute before saying, "You seem to know quite a bit more than you are telling me."

"We only know that you thought the painting might be valuable. Why else fly to Los Angeles. Unless, of course, you went for some other purpose, which would be a large coincidence."

"I do not have your painting, Mr. Wendel."

"I know you left Los Angeles without it." Now Wendel was winging it. Burgher might have stolen the painting and decided to keep his five million.

"Mr. Wendel, you own a painting that many people would like but cannot afford. Your Mr. Handler made clear that he could not sell me the painting because he didn't own it, and he also made clear that the owner, you, would want a lot more than the five million dollars our modest foundation could afford." Burgher reached for something as though he expected it to be on his desk, which contained nothing to reach for. From his pocket he took a pen—it looked like a fountain pen—and twiddled it. "I am not a killer or a thief. Before I knew anything about this painting, I circulated the picture Mr. Handler sent me in an effort to understand its origin. Some of the people who have seen it are not so righteous. I move easily in right wing circles and know that certain neo-Nazis imagine that the raised arm in the painting is meant to be part of a *sieg heil* salute. I am also welcome in communist circles where people believe the painting mocks the Nazis, much more likely given Herr Klee's attitude. To these groups the painting is priceless and warrants any means to obtain it. If you are wise, you will leave Switzerland without arousing any more curiosity than you already have."

Burgher stood up and walked around the desk. "Now I must end our conversation."

Wendel also stood, and Cheryl gathered her purse and jacket. Burgher led them to the front and told the receptionist to find his driver to take Wendel and Cheryl to their hotel. "The...where is it you said you were staying."

"The Schweizerhof," Wendel said and immediately wished he hadn't.

"Tell Hans to take Mr. and Mrs. Wendel to the Schweizerhof," Burgher said to the receptionist. "I must bid you good day."

As Burgher disappeared into the Entwurf's confines, Wendel wished he knew more about him. Was he a Nazi?

He certainly didn't fit Wendel's idea of a communist, not that he would have any realistic idea of how a Swiss communist would appear. Did the Swiss even have communists? Wendel would like to believe Burgher's interest was nothing more than as a foundation and museum manager, purely artistic. Apparently Burgher met with Handler but what did they talk about?

"You want to go with his driver?" Cheryl said. They stood near the door far enough away that the receptionist couldn't hear them.

"Why not. Might be hard to find a cab."

"Burgher gives me the creeps. We ought to be able to find a cab on the main street, Landenbergstrasse, I think it was."

"I told Burgher he was in the clear. He has nothing to worry about from us."

"Unless he hired someone to go back for the painting."

"Does he seem the type?"

"Who can tell? You know the Swiss."

"To Der Schweizerhof?" said a man who appeared through the same door Burgher had disappeared through. He looked large in a gray uniform-like jacket that was too small. Wendel's imagination immediately dredged up the image of Zvolens' helpers.

As soon as they were outside the man retrieved an unfamiliar-looking cigarette package, a European brand, from a pocket and lit up. In a Mercedes sedan that wasn't as comfortable as Wendel thought a car of its ilk should be, he slid the window half down and made an unsuccessful attempt to blow the smoke out. With each exhale some blew into the back seat, a strong aroma reminding Wendel of the Gitanes the French smoked. Cheryl coughed, maybe a real cough or maybe an attempt to make a point. Besides the cough, they were quiet as they drove through Lucerne's traffic.

The lake sparkled and rippled from a breeze. The Pedestrians' businesslike pace seemed out of sync with the peaceful life Wendel projected for an idyllic mountain environment like Lucerne. He wondered what heritage and psyche drove the Swiss in the same manner as the puritan ethic and commerce drove so many Americans. Calvinists he recalled from a college course. Hans stopped in front of the Schweizerhof as Wendel was thinking how nice it was going to be to stay a few days waiting for Zvolens to finish his business in Hungary.

"I will wait here while you pack your luggage," Hans said.

"We're not leaving," Wendel said.

"For your safety, Mr. Burgher says you will leave now. I will drive you to the Airport in Zurich."

They got out of the car and Wendel walked to Hans' window. "Thanks, but we can manage ourselves."

"I insist," the man said as Wendel turned to walk inside.

He turned back and said, "My friend cannot handle the smoke, but I appreciate the offer."

Up in the room Wendel tossed off the jacket and tugged at the necktie as he speed-dialed the European cell phone Zvolens had loaned him to keep in contact. Zvolens answered amidst what sounded like a party and went to another room to hear Wendel's report on Burgher and the Entwurf.

"I'll be another day or two," Zvolens said. "You could go down to Paris and see if you can learn anything at Handler's gallery." Like every other Zvolens' suggestion, this sounded more like an order than an option. Zvolens said to take the overnight train, that he'd book them a room the next night at the D'Aubusson on Rue Dauphine on the Left Bank and he'd pick them up at the Toussus-le-Noble Airport, wherever the hell that was, at four on Friday, two days hence. While Wendel stayed on the call, Zvolens tracked down and passed along the phone number of Handler's widow.

"To hell with Paris," Cheryl said after Wendel related Zvolens "suggestion." "I don't like Burgher, I don't like his driver, and I don't like these stupid beds. I'm going home."

"You'll love Paris," Wendel said. "We'll drop in on Handler's wife and then have a couple of days to ourselves."

"Burgher's right—Nazis and patriots are tracking us down. This is starting to sound like a Helen McGuinness novel."

"Who?" Wendel said.

"Never mind. You're not going to find that damn painting. It's hanging in someone's secret collection right now."

While Cheryl was in the bathroom, Wendel had the concierge book a double cabin on the overnight train from Zurich to Paris. They packed and checked out, Wendel picked up the train tickets in the lobby, and when they walked through the double doors to the street, Hans stood in front of the Mercedes. Wendel's first impulse was to find some way to avoid him. But then he guided Cheryl to the Mercedes and said, "Thanks for the advice. We'll walk to the station."

They rolled their bags as they retraced the day-before's route. "Is he following us?" Cheryl asked.

"I can't tell," Wendel said after looking over his shoulder. "We'll see when we get there."

As they boarded the train for Zurich, they didn't see Hans and hoped that by leaving they had satisfied whatever mission Burgher had given him. During the short ride Wendel told Cheryl about the overnight train, the trip to Paris and romance.

"I'm not in the mood for romance."

"We're both shaken up. We'll feel better after a night on the train.

"Shook up? Hell, I'm scared to death."

"We're okay now."

"Burgher threatened to kill us."

"If he wanted to kill us, he wouldn't warn us to get out of town. He'd put us off guard and then kill us."

Cheryl was quiet and after a moment leaned against him and tilted her head onto his shoulder. He tried to relax and make her feel comfortable, enjoying the feel of her soft hair against his cheek. After a few minutes he took and held her hand. Wendel marveled that he was talking about the chances of their being murdered as casually as he might talk about whether it might rain so that he ought to take an umbrella. He had been content as a small-time operator who occasionally stood a computer onto its ear.

People like Zvolens and Burgher who ran organizations and maneuvered in the world of big-time art, the kind of art he read about changing hands at Christy's or Sotheby's, made him uncomfortable

When Hans didn't turn up at the Zurich airport, Cheryl agreed to go to Paris. "It's still against my better judgment," she said.

"That'll change after a good meal with a smooth Burgundy on the Left Bank." Even as he said it, Wendel wasn't so sure that even Paris could reignite the playful Cheryl, the woman he shared a hot tub with and who had bantered aboard Zvolens's airplane about playing husband and wife. It would be a shame not to consummate their marriage in Paris before returning to LA for the annulment.

17

The overnight departed the Hauptbahnhof at 11 with their beds in the private compartment already made up. Twenty years ago Wendel would have gone for the chance to make love on the thin mattress that covered the narrow slab. Weird, uncomfortable, even contorted would have added to the romance. But now the too-narrow bed didn't inspire his fantasies. Better to wait until an evening in the Latin Quarter crept into their blood.

On the way to the toilette—the cabin had a basin but not a commode—Wendel smelled a pungent cigarette, maybe the same brand Hans had been smoking. He walked up and down the corridor but couldn't see into the compartments. The smell was weaker back a car and stronger forward so he walked to and through the non-sleeping cars. Still no sign of anyone resembling Hans. So he wandered back to his compartment where the latch secured them inside for the night. Cheryl, who had used the toilette before leaving the Hauptbahnhof, was in the lower berth with her most relaxed look of the day. He didn't tell her about the cigarette. Instead he sat beside her, nudged her to roll over and massaged her back and shoulders while she encouraged him with soft moans. Lightly he ran his fingers through the fuzz on her back at her waist, and resisted an urge to travel down between her thighs. He'd wait for tomorrow. Despite the narrowness of the upper berth, he slept until the conductor roused them as they rolled through the outskirts of Paris.

"Bonjour. We are delighted to have you stay with us," said the receptionist at the D'Aubusson. Was she especially cheerful because of Zvolens or did she greet all guests with such warmth? It was too early to check in but she promised to have their bags in "la chamber superior" by mid afternoon. Handler's gallery was around the corner on Rue Mazarine. His widow, Ginette, lived upstairs and had agreed to meet for breakfast at a cafe on St. Germaine des Pres where they ordered cappuccinos and croissants.

"It was a big loss," she said in response to Cheryl's intuitive expression of empathy. "The loss is in affection. We have not been lovers for years."

"Still a shock," Wendel said, and after she nodded and they sipped their coffees, he added, "Are you going to continue the gallery?"

"Oh yes. I share Jean's ardor for aiding les jeunes artistes, a tradition most galleries have left behind with their high-priced expectations."

"How did Jean happen to have a special interest in Paul Klee?" Wendel asked.

"He didn't. Eighty years ago Jean would have celebrated Klee, maybe even discovered him, but now he would have only a passing interest. He put so much of himself into his artists. Les inconnus were his passion."

"Some people think I own a previously undiscovered Klee," Wendel said. "I'm sure that would have drawn his attention, at least enough to figure out whether my three-dollar print was an original watercolor."

"Peut-etre. Because he was on vacation and needed something to do. Jean needed to be busy. But he didn't mention the Klee to me when we talked."

Ginette drank her espresso with the French touch that made it last forever while Wendel's cup was almost empty. After they sat quietly for a few minutes, he asked if she knew Burgher. Except for having received a call from Monsieur Burgher asking where her husband was staying in LA, Ginette couldn't place the man, even when Wendel mentioned the Entwurf.

"You could easily forget him," Cheryl said, "unless you made him uncomfortable and he sent his driver for you."

"We can check the Rolodex at the gallery," Ginette said.

Wendel and Cheryl both indulged second croissants, the chocolate ones that had come with the batch. Wendel savored how the roll flaked in his mouth and resented how automatically the French had learned not to overeat their rich food. Food might be important but not as important as la figure. Still they seemed to have much fatter Achilles tendons than Americans, the kind of thing he noticed when he traveled alone but kept to himself not wanting to reveal what some would call a fetish.

When they walked to the gallery, the sidewalks were crowded even though the early rush was over. Inside were the same weird pieces Wendel had observed when he had been in Paris two weeks earlier. The thought of two weeks startled him. It felt more like two years.

Burgher was not in the Rolodex. Nor was the Ent-wurf. "This does not mean anything," Ginette said. "Jean knew many people he didn't keep in this thing." She tapped the cards as she spoke. "These days it is so easy to find someone on the web."

"I'm intrigued by this one painting," Wendel said, pointing toward one that actually looked like a recognizable landscape. "It doesn't resemble anything else you have here."

"Oh, that is Cherbet's first painting. We can sell it for a great deal because now he is dead and they do retrospectives—she said the word with the French emphasis on the last syllable—and need this painting to show his development. Have you not seen the boy and the horse by Picasso at your Museum of Modern Art in New York? Even if it were not so perfect it would be valuable to show from where Picasso came."

They walked around the gallery as Ginette told them about each of the artists and what made them avant-garde. "Maybe you would like to buy something, help a young artist. Who knows, maybe someone will think it is valuable enough to steal in another fifty years."

"Let's buy one together," Cheryl said. "The beginning of our collection."

"Do you think we can agree on one?"

"Not yesterday when we were married, but probably today," she said. "You pick."

Wendel pointed to a canvas with a botch of colors that had a modicum of appeal including that it was under three hundred Euros, less than most the others. "We'll keep this in your house," he said.

"Splendid. I'd love it. Who knows, we might merge collections someday."

"If you do," Ginette said, "I recommend that you keep separate houses. The best medicine for a strong relationship."

Wendel pulled out his credit card and by the time Ginette figured the lousy Euro-Dollar exchange rate, the cost came to almost five hundred dollars. He decided not to bargain—Handler had always bargained with customers—rationalizing that he wanted to help the artist and Ginette. Trouble was Cheryl, who needed ten thousand dollars, probably couldn't pay her share, and he'd soon have his own financial problems if he didn't stop playing detective and get back to work walking computers, which is what he called his profession, kind of like what dog sitters did. At least, he noticed, he could silently rejoice over Ginette's fat Achilles tendons and Cheryl's return to playfulness.

Before leaving Wendel searched online for galleries that handled Klee paintings and then took a look at his emails. Receiving none of interest made him feel lonely, wanting to extend his trip with Cheryl. Because that wasn't possible, he fished his flash storage from his pocket and sent out an email inviting the usual group to his house next Sunday for breakfast and gospel church.

He and Cheryl spent the day drinking espresso and looking at art. While they walked Cheryl said, "Strange that Handler emailed Burgher if he hardly knew him."

"Once he realized I had an original watercolor, he needed to find someone who knew something about Klee. He tried Zvolens who wasn't available. Maybe he didn't even know Burgher but found him on the Internet."

"I might have seen Burgher at your house one day when I dropped by, let myself in off your patio, but left once I heard voices. I didn't pay attention to whomever Handler was talking to, though I think he had an accent."

"That's news," Wendel said. "Any idea what they were talking about?"

"Might have been art, but maybe I assume that because of what's happened."

Wendel swallowed a piece of dark chocolate that had been dissolving in his mouth and also swallowed a comment about Handler's facility with the women from Wendel's life, not that Margo was a woman in his life or Cheryl for that matter, though both now qualified as former wives.

Back in the D'Aubisson, they lay down to rest before dinner. Wendel began to massage Cheryl's feet and then her back, which she reinforced with the appropriate murmurs. Before he could become more intimate, she was asleep, which made him wonder if he had a special facility for touch, maybe the key to a new profession as a massage therapist if his consulting went south. He rolled onto his back and next thing he knew she was rubbing his feet, though she wasn't as good at it as he considered himself. Still he welcomed the touch. After a while he unbuttoned her blouse and she took off her bra.

In a few minutes she said, "Let's go for that dinner you were talking about and come back early. It will be kind of nice to eat something special, something French, and have some good wine while we remember how we feel right now."

"You're the master of anticipation," he said.

"Anticipation can be as nice as love-making and makes the love-making all the more exciting."

True but Wendel was more than ready. In the name of anticipation he resisted self-satisfaction while in the shower. Dressed and on the street, they strolled to I'le de St. Louis and the intimate bistro the concierge had recommended. La Petite Blanche Fleur with its fresh vegetables was like Chez Panisse in Berkeley, a comparison, he figured, that no French restaurant would want, even if the French enjoyed fresh vegetables as much as Californians.

After Wendel turned to accept a morsel Cheryl put slowly into his mouth, he swallowed and said, "Good foreplay if it weren't for the fact that the guy at the bar over your shoulder—don't turn now—looks familiar."

"Everyone looks familiar when you're traveling," she said. "People always look like someone I know."

"I could swear I saw him today, outside one of the galleries."

"Now who's getting paranoid. If he's following us, he's putting a damn good meal on his expense account."

The chocolate cake was irresistible, so they carried a piece in a napkin to split the next day. As they wandered back over the Pont St. Louis and past the backside of Notre Dame where the street was dark, Wendel glanced over his shoulder. The man at the bar was following. Wendel passed this information on to Cheryl and took her arm to move them along. He thought they could reach the lighted front of Notre Dame, full of sightseers, before the man caught up, even if he started to run.

"What now," Cheryl said as they merged with a group listening to a tour guide.

"Let's stand here with these people and see what he does." Only then did Wendel realize the group was all Japanese. That ought to give Hans or whomever else Burgher sent after them a laugh. Meanwhile he could enjoy hearing how Bishop-this and Pope-that built the massive structure, how the bell weighed thirteen tons.

"Gives me more respect for Peter Lorre," Wendel said.

"Who's that?"

"He played the Hunchback and rang the bell."

"Lon Cheney you mean."

"I'm sure it was Lorre,"

"Or Charles Laughton or Anthony Hopkins," she said.

"Whoever, they all get my respect."

"What's he doing?"

"I'm going to kiss you," he said, "so I can look over your shoulder inconspicuously."

They shared one of those seemingly-endless, tongue exploring kisses, which made Wendel forget to take a good look around, so they kissed again, which revealed the man standing near another group of tourists, and also inspired murmurs of appreciation by the Japanese as well as flashes from their cameras.

"He's still here," Wendel said.

"Any ideas?"

"I remember a Metro stop nearby. I see the sign. We can pull the old trick of getting on and then off at the last second leaving him on."

"And if he gets off, then maybe he and we are the only people left on the platform."

"I could push him onto the tracks."

"These people here seem to like us. Maybe we could catch a ride when they leave."

Wendel told the tour guide that someone was following them and asked if they could go on their bus to their next stop. The woman spoke Japanese to the group and the idea brought oohs and aahs and approval.

"I'm afraid all the woman will want me to kiss them," he said.

"Not to worry," the tour guide said.

Shortly the group headed toward one of the buses waiting nearby where inside the guide insisted they take the front seat next to her. Out the window the man who was following them watched as they drove off. The guide told them that they were headed to the Moulin Rouge in Montmartre, which might not be the best place to catch a Metro at night, but if they stayed with the group and took some seats of people who hadn't come that night, the next stop after the Follies would be the Latin Quarter for a good-night dessert. This made Wendel realize he had been squeezing their chocolate cake he was still holding, and before he could answer, Cheryl accepted the invitation.

"It might be too late to make love," he whispered.

"Make love? After all this? You think you're James Bond?"

Wendel said the Follies might stimulate their desire, but Cheryl didn't answer. In fact the Follies had no such effect. It was a great floorshow with more outstanding tits than he'd seen in a lifetime, which wasn't saying much, yet the presentation was hardly sensual. At intermission they carried glasses of Champagne onto the street and smiled at their Japanese friends. Cheryl and Wendel had released enough of their tension that Cheryl accepted his arm around her waist and escort up the street away from the crowd. At the corner they turned and looked back.

Suddenly he felt the presence of someone behind him. Before he could turn, a hand reached around him and grabbed his crotch. He felt like he jumped five feet and let out a yell. "Voulez-vous l'amour?" a woman said.

He didn't need his high school French to know that question. Awareness that she was a woman of the night registered more quickly than his fear let go so that even when he knew he hadn't been accosted by the man following them, his adrenaline surged. His desire also surged, a credit to Cheryl rather than the prostitute, he rationalized.

"Not tonight," Cheryl said.

"Le menage a trios est tres fantastique," the woman said.

"Tempting," Wendel said as he steered them back to the theater to join the others returning to their seats.

"Some other time," Cheryl added over her shoulder.

When the bus dropped them next at Cafe Les Deux Magots, the guide invited them to join the group even though they would have to make their own choices because the cost wasn't covered in the prepaid price. By now Wendel, who hadn't entirely tuned his internal clock with European time, was no longer tired so why not have a coffee and dessert. In fact he told the guide that he wanted to put the bill for the entire group on his credit card, which after some discussion, the leader graciously accepted. He didn't regret his gesture even when he saw the healthy prices. The chocolate cake was a mess so they shared a tort.

Wide awake, he eventually escorted Cheryl down Rue Dauphine ready to re-entice her into their long-anticipated lovemaking. As they neared the hotel he slowed and searched for the man they had said goodbye to at Notre Dame, but he was not in sight. The hotel was locked and the night clerk let them in and retrieved their key. In the cozy elevator Wendel stood behind Cheryl who willingly let him hold her against his body. By the time they inched to the fifth floor—the elevator's speed was akin to climbing hand over hand—Cheryl commented that she could tell what he had in mind and that she was right with him.

The light that came on automatically when he swung open the door to their room revealed the man who had been following them, sitting in the room's easy chair, one leg crossed over the other.

18

Before Wendel could say, "what the hell" or "merde," he saw the man held a gun. Wendel might have ducked out, but Cheryl was already in the room and would never have made it.

"Attende," the man said. "Je suis un ami."

"I think he said, 'friend,'" Wendel said.

The man rattled off more French and Wendel heard, "Zvolens." He also put the gun away.

"Slower," Wendel said. "Lentement s'il vous plait. Je parle un peu de Francais."

It took five minutes but Wendel was pretty sure Zvolens had hired the man, Joseph, to protect them. Despite Wendel's protests Joseph was going to spend the night in their easy chair. Someone, who fit the description of Hans, had followed them during the day. This man had not threatened them—had only kept an eye on them. Still the man might be waiting for the right moment, so Joseph settled into the chair and claimed he wouldn't disturb them. Yeah sure, Wendel thought. Not that it mattered. Finding the guy in their room had routed his passion.

On the plus side Wendel was physically and emotionally exhausted and slept through the night. The next day Joseph accompanied them and suggested a couple of museums as well as the best chocolate in Paris, "absolument le mieux." No sign of Hans, and then Joseph drove them to Toussus-le-Noble Airport. The perpetually effer-vescent Zvolens greeted them with west-coast hugs and after chatting with Joseph and handing him a fistful of Euros, followed Wendel and Cheryl up the stairs into the Hawker 1000.

After takeoff Zvolens apologized for getting them into a tight spot, an apology that lost some of its luster when he repeated his "expectation" that Wendel go to Idaho.

"You have a bodyguard on retainer in Coeur d'Alaine like Paris?" Wendel said.

"I wish I did," Zvolens said. "You need to be very careful there."

Zvolens suggested they review what they knew about the murder suspects. Burgher headed the list even though he would have had to hire someone to kill Handler after returning to Switzerland. And then why would he kill Gorman? Were Burgher and Gorman neo-Nazis? They sat quietly and eventually had to admit that they had no idea.

"Maybe Burgher killed Handler and someone else killed Gorman," Cheryl said.

Her comment reminded Wendel that the Chief con-sidered him a prospect for Gorman's murder. They talked about how the Hammer was in the neighborhood around the time of both murders, and Wendel noted that so was Brendan, though he couldn't conceive of Brendan as a murderer.

"He had access, and as a former Seal, he certainly had the ability," Zvolens said. "He probably killed a few people while he was in the Navy."

"But what's his motive?" Wendel said.

Wendel wondered why he didn't bring up Margo, as though he were trying to protect her. She had been uncharacteristically likeable the week before when exposure of her tryst with Handler made her vulnerable to losing both her marriage and her job. Hard to picture Handler blackmailing Margo, yet he might have suggested it would be in her interest to use the family wealth to support his unknown artists.

"Maybe Gorman killed Handler," Zvolens said, "which means there had to be a second murderer."

"Probably his wife," Wendel said.

"Or you," Zvolens said. "Revenge for killing your friend and stealing your painting."

"Yeah right," Wendel said. "Maybe it was Cheryl or the Chief of police."

"Don't get testy," Zvolens said. "Whoever killed him, maybe the Hammer, probably deserves a medal." They discussed Wendel's trip to Idaho and when Cheryl stressed the need to be careful, Wendel appreciated that the danger inspired her concern.

While they refueled in Gander, they trotted out their cell phones. Wendel's only message was from Sally Simms at GeTechNome asking him to proceed with the implementation of the system trials.

"Good news," he said to Cheryl and told her about the call. He saw that her mind was elsewhere, and said, "What's up."

"I had a call from Trent."

"Trent?"

"The man I met at Esalen."

"Warbucks."

"He wants me to spend next week at his place in Tahoe."

"But we're supposedly married."

"It's not funny," she said. "I'm torn. He's a nice guy and I'd have money for the rest of my life, but am I ready to settle for an uninspiring nice guy?"

"Beats an inspiring ass hole," Wendel said, and wished he hadn't because he too was unsettled. Cheryl might see him as an uninspiring nice guy who wasn't rich. Or worse as an uninspiring ass hole. "What are you going to do?" he said.

"I don't know."

What she did know and told him was that she needed to figure it out and was going to spend the night alone after they got home. After so many times coming close to sex with Cheryl, Wendel saw they might never make it together. He attached his flash storage to the "guest PC" Zvolens carried on the plane and sublimated by checking his computer program for the GeTechNome experiment. An hour before they landed he fell asleep, and by the time they set down on the Long Beach runway, he was wide-awake.

He called the Chief to see if he and Cheryl could come in and report on the trip, but the Chief had left for the day and Wendel opted not to call the emergency number. Without Gorman paying the bills, the security service had disappeared from the entry to their lane, which Wendel mildly regretted—he enjoyed fetching food for two rather than just himself. Instead he ate a peanut butter, lettuce, tomato and sardine sandwich. Most people gagged when he described this combo, even though he tried to persuade whomever he could to give it a try.

He finally got to sleep about five in the morning and the phone woke him at seven. Margo said she was sorry to call so early but rain had cancelled her husband's golf game and he wanted Wendel to come for an interview at 8:30 at their home in Bel Air. Howard might want to hire Wendel who needed the money even though he questioned whether he could work with a self-impressed CEO known for jerking people around. At a seminar one IT vice president had told Wendel how his boss at an aerospace company had demanded his attention until ten minutes before his 747 departed for a European vacation and then had him limoed across the airport runways to join his wife who had no idea whether she was flying to Greece alone. When they got home, the VP discovered that either god or the CEO—what was the difference?—had deposited $25,000 in his bank account "to cover the cost of the vacation."

Taylor's home—Wendel made a silent bet that Margo wasn't on the title—was a sprawling enclosure that made the new homes on Wendel's block resemble servants' quarters. Margo met him at the door and shooed the maid away.

"Howard knows about Handler and me," she said.

"What happened?"

"I didn't tell you, but I hired a private detective who came up with some pretty good videos of him. After that policeman questioned me about Handler, I decided to confront Howard before he found out anything about me. When I did, he said that's just how it is and if I didn't like it, he'd give me a divorce and pay me the ten million specified in our pre-nuptial agreement. Or I could have my own frolics as he called them. So I told him about Handler."

"Big shots don't necessarily believe turnabout is fair play."

"He's fine. He even admired how I hired the detective and confronted him before making my confession, said this firmed up a decision he'd been considering to put me in charge of his motion picture studio. He said I'd keep my job if we split. Business comes first."

Wendel felt like saying that he should have asked for alimony, but instead said, "I'm happy for you." Still he suspected that a clever man like Taylor might pretend to accept Margo's tryst while planning his revenge. He marveled how anyone could work for someone like Taylor, much less be married to him, and realized that he still didn't understand his former wife. Wendel imagined being summoned by Taylor at five in the morning to collect his fee, ringing the doorbell, punching Taylor in the nose and walking out without the check. This image provoked a sudden fear of how violence had taken over his fantasies, as though surviving Zvolens' henchman and escaping from Hans in Lucerne had made him a fighter. "In this corner," he could hear being announced, "with a record of zero and zero, is Wendel the challenger."

"It was kind of fun being in our old house," Margo said.

"The old seductive Margo," Wendel said, wondering if she could be this cavalier after having killed Handler.

"Are you interested? she said.

"I'm involved with someone, and we're not as complex as you and your husband." He was surprised at how glibly he turned his three days traveling with Cheryl into being involved, probably provoked by anxiety over being drawn into Margo's orbit.

Margo led him through an overly chintzed and cushioned living room, past a dining table that could sit King Arthur's entourage plus wives and children, a den that actually looked used and habitable with computers aglow, papers on two different desks, and comfortable chairs, and then into a gym where a man, presumably Howard Taylor, was riding one of those stationary bikes that jerked him around. While pedaling and undulating he was watching three of the fifteen or so TV sets built into the walls. With his head Taylor motioned them to sit on a piece of exercise equipment with a movable carriage about two feet off the floor, which Margo said was a Pilates Reformer but looked like a medieval rack.

Taylor toweled some sweat off his face and said, "I need to tie all my companies into one computer system so I can keep track without asking."

"Your empire has a reputation of being so well run I'm surprised it's not already integrated," Wendel said as he dug his shoes into the carpet to keep the Pilates platform from sliding.

"I've acquired companies faster than we've been able to assimilate them."

"I once tied a group together," Wendel said, "much smaller but the approach would be the same."

Taylor asked intelligent questions, showing more knowledge about IT than Wendel would have guessed. As with the computers Wendel mastered, he multi-tasked, so while he schmoozed Taylor, he registered his own reactions. For example he realized that a sweating, twisting, undulating Taylor retained a commanding presence.

"Tell me about your company, Wendell."

"My company is me. I plan and oversee the kind of project you want. Systems I design are easily usable by non-tech people. I either subcontract implementation or work with whomever you hire."

"Sounds a little thin," Taylor said. Understandable from someone who had parlayed a home-shopping cable network into a multi-media conglomerate of newspapers, magazines, education and entertainment TV, and recently a securities dealer.

"Thin by design because systems concocted by committee incorporate too many bad ideas. You have plenty of expertise in your companies to challenge and second-guess me."

Taylor slowed to a cool-down pace and turned on eight more TVs, probably his own channels, none as bright as his ego. Wendel knew from Margo that a day a month Taylor volunteered anonymously at a homeless shelter where he handed out towels, cooked meals, washed dishes, kind of like the incongruity a few years back when an asshole conservative op-ed contributor joined Wendel's softball team and turned out to be a personable, people-oriented, charitable guy.

Taylor said Wendel came with a good reference from Margo, that he was interviewing more people, and that he'd let Wendel know. As all three of them walked to door, Wendel handed over a list of client references.

"By the way," Wendel said before leaving. He explained his "church" service and invited them to his house the next day. "You'd appreciate the gospel group, might even hire them for one of your networks. The band has some fabulous musicians from around LA."

Wendel grabbed a cappuccino in Westwood and sat back and relaxed. Around him a young couple talked in earnest, a group of women debated a marketing plan, an architect presented plans to a client, and sounds from several other business meetings wafted his way, beaucoup activity for a Saturday. No wonder Americans were good at business. These people were Wendel of twenty years earlier, and like him back then, they probably believed they would always be doing what they were doing today. Their ideas would never feel stale, their IRAs would rival Jack's bean stalk. An "old guy" came in, and then Wendel realized that he and the man were about the same age. An email from Brendan said he was coming to church and bringing the Hammer.

He called the Chief to leave him a message and was surprised to find him in the office on Saturday. After Wendel related what happened in Europe, the Chief said, "Burgher probably killed him and has your picture, and there's not a thing I can do about it." He sounded about as disappointed as he would over losing a two-dollar bet at Santa Anita.

"What next?" Wendel said.

"I have the records of all the phone calls on your line while you were on vacation," the Chief said. "Plus all calls on Handler's cell."

"Any I can check on?"

"Stay out of it. We'll follow up."

Wendel resented that the Chief used him to fly to Lucerne and then shut him out. Still he was relieved. After church tomorrow he would have plenty to do with GeTechNome on Monday and then he'd be off to Idaho.

Before hanging up he said, "I'm having church Sunday morning at the house. I've invited all the suspects except for Burgher. Come on over and find the killer."

The Chief's response sounded like a yawn.

Wendel picked up some bagels and sweet rolls for his guests and headed home. After exiting the 405 and winding through Manhattan Beach and Hermosa Beach, he came up behind a Corvair like the one that Waldo Peterson drove. At least it was in front of him this time, though Wendel wondered if maybe it had been following him in LA. His paranoia amused him, that is until the Corvair turned left across from Wendel's lane, the same place he had first seen it. Maybe whoever was following him hung out there waiting to see where Wendel went.

He turned in after the car and followed it around a bend, right at a corner and then left into a cul-de-sac. Slowly he wound around the semi-circle and as he headed back out saw Waldo Peterson get out of the Corvair and walk toward the house.

"Waldo," he called out after rolling down the window. "I didn't know we were neighbors."

Peterson walked back toward the street where they chatted a few minutes, Wendel explaining that he lived across Highland.

"What are you doing here in the low rent area?" Peterson said.

"I saw you and wanted to be sure you got the invitation for church tomorrow at my house. The gospel service I told you about."

19

When Wendel called Cheryl Sunday morning about sharing the hot tub before church, he got no answer. She might already be in the tub, so he wrapped himself into his cherry cloth robe, grabbed his phone and headed for the patio. A note on the tub cover greeted him.

"My dear Wendel, Last night I couldn't sleep and wanted to use my key to let myself in and crawl into your bed. I couldn't get my mind off Trent and don't know why. I'm frightened that I'll trade what I want for security, which I've never worried about before. Am I getting old?

"I've decided to go away to a Buddhist monastery up the coast with rooms for visitors on silent retreats. I can't reach them until later, but I'm driving up betting they can take me for a week. I don't know what will come of this, but I hope you'll have patience for my daffiness and will understand. I loved our short marriage, which we may someday consummate.

"With love, Cheryl."

Sitting in the hot tub Wendel realized he'd need to be reincarnated before he could follow Buddha's example of quiet contemplation at a silent retreat. The current iteration of Wendel couldn't survive a day of silence. He had once tried three days at a monastery near Carmel and bolted after a lunch of nuts and raisons on the first day, finishing the retreat at Ventana, a new-age resort with plenty of conversation in the no-bathing-suit section of the spa. A week's silent retreat would be impressive if Cheryl could do it. But what would it tell her about him?

The band arrived before 9:00 and while they found their spots on the patio and the drummer set up, Wendel taped a copy of the Klee onto the wall next to where they would be playing. Wendel always began the "service" with a two-minute homily, which today he would dedicate to the safe whereabouts and return of the painting. One of the guests might know something about it.

Some bikers announced their arrival by trying to blow out their mufflers and then took over setting up chairs from the garage while Wendel stoked two coffee urns and set out the sweet rolls and bagels. When Brendan and the Hammer arrived, the Hammer waved off Brendan's intro.

"I know the man," the Hammer said.

"How'd Cal do yesterday?" Wendel said.

"On a roll, baby. Movin' up in the polls."

"You knew my neighbor, Gorman, who was murdered?" Wendel asked.

The Hammer neither flinched nor broke stride as he said, "Knew the guy for years. Bought a few guns from him."

"Any idea who might have killed him?" Wendel asked.

"A lot of people didn't like him," the Hammer said. "Including you."

Before Wendel could scoff, Brendan said, "The three of us are riding north together on Tuesday. The Hammer has invited us to his Coeur D'Alene home."

Wendel continued to set up and looked for a chance to speak with Brendan alone about why he kept turning up with the Hammer. Wendel wouldn't have guessed they were a compatible couple. A little before ten Gloria Gorman strolled in, looking right and left until her gaze fell onto Wendel, and then she bird-dogged toward him. He girded for the Gorman rant her husband used to deliver about the up-coming "clamor."

"Thanks so much for including me," she said. "I've always listened from our den, but Henry never let me come."

Wendel made it a point to invite the neighbors who, except for Cheryl, stayed away. Gloria's liberation inspired him to give her a hug. Maybe she had killed Gorman, he thought, recalling he had said as much as a joke a few days earlier. He introduced her to some bikers, some of whom were familiar with her husband's former company, and excused himself to check on the choir most of whom were still sitting around drinking coffee and eating bagels. He poured a cup and was about to sit until Sally Simms and Waldo Peterson walked in.

"We want to see if this church thing is the source of your creativity," Sally said.

"My motorcycle fills that role," he said. "Church is spiritual inspiration."

"Great old house," Peterson said.

"Look around." Wendel told them he was installing the system before going north for a few days and that when he got back, they'd begin the pilot program for the scientists to try.

We're ready," Peterson said actually sounding enthusiastic. "Do you keep a big main frame here for programming?"

"I can program on a PC," Wendel said and was about to entertain them with the story of how he was flying without any computer these days when he saw Brendan walk into the kitchen and excused himself.

"What's with you and the Hammer?" he said. "The two of you turn up together every time there's a murder."

"Who do you think we're after today?" Brendan said.

"The Hammer might be after someone, and I'm guessing the Chief of police has his eye on both of you. I wouldn't have thought you were friends."

"He's okay. Hates the government but lots of people do."

The government represented the kind of authority Wendel hated as well but it was either too large or too obvious a target for his rebellious nature. He wasn't going to direct his dislike at a cliche. CEOs like Howard Taylor worked better, he thought as he saw Taylor and Margo walk in off the patio. Margo must have led them through the side gate.

"How about you?" Wendel asked Brendan. "Do you hate the government?"

"They pay my pension," Brendan said. "I can't hate them too much for letting me live this life. I know you want to check out the Hammer and I thought you could begin on the drive north. You okay with that?"

Wendel imagined Brendan as his body guard if the Hammer got rough. Before Wendel shook loose, Margo brought her husband into the kitchen where she found a couple of mugs for their coffee.

"Paper not good enough?" Wendel said, ignoring, at least for the moment, his irritation that she knew where he kept the mugs, and wishing he had moved them since she departed or installed a punching bag on a spring to pop her in the nose when she opened the cabinet.

"We're environmentalists," she said.

"Save the paper and use the detergent," Brendan said before introducing himself.

"Come meet the choir," Wendel said resisting the urge to utter something that would cost him Taylor's IT business. He led them to the living room and left them to talk with the band and choir about the entertainment world.

Shortly all the guests moved to the patio where Wendel was surprised to see Zvolens talking with the Hammer. Could he have flown down from Salinas just for Wendel's church? The choir sang for an hour while the band gradually amped the sound. Wendel missed having Cheryl to share the vibes. He ought to do this every week. Toward the end of the show Chief Pruett walked through the side door and stood next to Wendel, who wondered if the Chief was responding to neighborhood complaints. Back when Gorman had sued Wendel over the noise, a sympathetic judge had ruled that the First Amendment to the Constitution protected the church service, and that after all, many churches were in residential areas. Occasional loud noise from Wendel on Sunday morning was no greater a nuisance than conventional churches' bell-ringing all week and outpouring of people at the end of services.

But the Chief said nothing about the noise. Instead when the band finished and Wendel started toward the front to give his homily, the Chief grabbed his arm and walked ahead of him.

"Party's over folks, " he said. "Someone murdered one of the neighbors a couple weeks ago. We've found what we believe is the murder weapon, a tire iron, maybe from a motor cycle repair kit. Two LA County detectives are standing outside with your motor cycles to collect DNA. We'll be taking buccal swabs, which is harmless so you have nothing to fear unless you killed someone. So walk out front next to your cycle, we'll take the swabs and you can be on your way or continue to party."

The dead Gorman could only have dreamed of the silence that settled on the patio. All Wendel heard were the birds Cheryl fed in her yard. After a few minutes muted conversation returned as the guests murmured with each other about what this all meant.

Wendel didn't have to talk with anyone. He remembered the day the Chief confiscated his motor cycle tools but not his tire iron. Intuitively he knew someone had stolen the iron with the sharpened end and used it to kill Gorman. Slowly the cyclists walked through the house to where the deputies were waiting. Wendel started to follow and at the front door ran into Margo and Taylor.

"Will he want my DNA?" Margo said.

"Probably. I'm sure he'll want mine. Let's find out."

"I don't have a motorcycle and I never knew the victim," Taylor said while giving Margo what seemed to

Wendel to be an amused look. "Stay if you want but I'm leaving before the paparazzi arrive. Wendel can give you a ride. On his motorcycle."

Wendel and Margo watched Taylor walk out and point to his Lamborghini that was slung so low it looked like a snake would have an easier time getting in than Taylor. The Chief waved him on. "I have your plate if I need to reach you Mr. Taylor," he said. Not bad, Wendel thought as he watched Taylor bend and swing in with almost one motion for which he probably trained by doing yoga and a half dozen other California-type therapies.

"Let's just do it," Wendel said to Margo. "You'll make him suspicious if you try to avoid it."

The swabs resembled tongue depressants, which reminded Wendel of how his pediatrician gave him the used one to propel spit balls, and then his mother would take it away in the car. The swabs had a rough finish and the deputies ran one back and forth eight times on the inside of his cheek and then ran another eight times inside the other cheek.

Wendel considered the Hammer the most likely candidate to have set him up. If the Hammer was the one, he wasn't making any special effort to avoid the swabs. Why should he? Traces of Wendel's blood from his leg wound were probably on the tire iron while the Hammer neither spit nor bled on the damn thing when he killed Gorman. If it was the Hammer.

Zvolens volunteered his own DNA sample even though he had a rental car and no bike. He buttonholed Wendel before returning to the airport.

"Be careful in Idaho," he said. "I've looked into your Mr. Hammer. Killed a man 15 years ago. He got off with voluntary manslaughter and a year in prison. Still claims he's innocent. The so-called false conviction is why he hates the government."

Wendel wanted to cancel Idaho, except now he had to go to find evidence against the Hammer before the Chief got the DNA results and arrested Wendel. He assured Zvolens he'd be careful.

"I can't find much about your friend, Wilde, since he left the navy, but he was no prince there. A regular troublemaker, always challenging his superiors' authority." Wendel had no trouble believing this description. "The Seals got tired of him even though he was a first-class soldier."

After Zvolens drove off Wendel wanted to call his lawyer but needed to get these people out of his house. He asked Brendan if he'd give Margo a ride home, told Margo he had to get ready to leave town and that she'd enjoy holding onto Brendan's bod. He was relieved that the Hammer went with them. One of the bikers and a couple of choir members insisted on helping him clean up and he felt compelled to open and share a bottle of wine. Finally about 2 he reached the attorney who had helped him with his tax problems and got the name of Demetrius Snider, a criminal lawyer.

"Don't ever hire a criminal lawyer who's not available on Sunday," Snider said when Wendel called him.

"I appreciate that," Wendel said. "Here's my problem."

"Hold it. Not over the phone until we find out if it's the kind of situation the authorities might have you bugged over. Hello J. Edgar. For years I've said hello to Mr. Hoover whom I assume has found a way in hell to keep listening. I'll meet you in my office in an hour, Mr. Wendel."

The address Snider gave him was in Little Tokyo, "the perfect place for a Greek lawyer" was how Snider put it, "near the LA county building and the courts." Wendel was early which gave him time to wolf down some sushi and wander through an exhibit of eighteen life-sized paper mache flying hippopotami in the Temporary Contemporary Museum. The exhibit seemed about as plausible as his present life, which made him wonder if this was the artist's intent regarding the present lives of contemporary humans.

"Who didn't you kill?" Snider said after unlocking his office and leading him in "By the way I'm $500.00 an hour, nothing extra for Sunday."

With that information Wendel told the story of the last couple weeks in under eight minutes.

Snider sat quietly for a while after Wendel finished and then said, "You ought to tell that policeman that this tire iron might be yours. That will give you more credibility with the jury than if you wait for the DNA to come back."

"He might arrest me."

"Probably will. We can arrange bail in advance."

"How much?" Wendel asked.

"Maybe a million. Cost you $100,000 unless you have property with a million of equity."

"Maybe. Maybe not. I'm going to Idaho Tuesday."

"I can only recommend," Snider said. "Do what you have to." Maybe it was Wendel's imagination but Snider seemed to lose enthusiasm when Wendel wasn't sure about the amount of equity in his house. Might not be anything left over to pay his fee. Snider began to look through papers on his desk and spun his chair around to search in a cabinet behind him.

Wendel said he'd think about it and Snider agreed to arrange the bail if and when, provided Wendel could first write a $50,000 retainer check. "Today's on me," Snider said. "I had to pick up a file anyway."

"How long until the DNA comes back?" Wendel asked.

"A week, maybe two."

A generous guy, Wendel thought as he walked to his car without writing a $250.00 check for the half-hour visit. He had a week to find the killer or suffer the consequences of being a fugitive, which would not endear him to GeTechNome, Howard Taylor or any other client. He'd need Gorman to return from the dead to buy his house so he could pay a good lawyer. On the drive home he was haunted by the image of becoming some guy's wife in San Quentin.

20

"We're going Highway 1," the Hammer said. "I've never seen Big Sur." The route was okay, the Hammer giving orders was not. Wendel wondered if he'd make it as far as Coeur D'Alene without popping off.

They each tossed out some money to cover breakfast at one of those places where you squeeze onto a bench at a long table with strangers. The Hammer and Brendan left Wendel to figure out the tip, and he soon realized the Hammer's contribution might not even cover the tax, much less something for the waitress.

Driving north, Wendel couldn't get his mind off the coming GeTechNome tests. He had spent the day before at the company checking out his programs that the IT department could tie into their work while he was gone so they could begin the trials when he got back. He should have merged the programs himself, but he couldn't stay focused with the Hammer and Idaho on his mind.

They pushed up highways 101 and 1, and Brendan urged them past Hearst Castle with a guarantee of a fabulous ride at Fort Hunter Liggett, assuming the Hammer wasn't on the unwelcome list for military bases. They cleared the security gate and searched for something called South Coast Ridge Road, which rose above the Pacific through a series of narrow switchbacks. A car met them coming around a curve and the Hammer swerved out of the way, almost forcing Wendel over the edge.

When they paused on a cliff overlooking the ocean, Wendel said, "You didn't have to cut in front of me."

"You're probably right," the Hammer said. "Have you noticed your rear tire's a little low. Is that the one you patched the day I met you in Pozo?"

Wendel took a look and agreed it was a shade low. "After Gorman's murder, the Chief of Police took all my tools. I need to borrow a CO_2 cartridge to see if it the tire will hold."

"At least you don't have to worry that the murder weapon they found is yours," Brendan said.

"Unless someone stole it to commit the murder," Wendel said.

The Hammer shifted from his right foot to his left to steady his Harley. He looked out at the ocean as though he hadn't heard the end of the conversation.

"How the hell can you stab someone with a tire iron?" Brendan said while he filled Wendel's tire.

Wendel said nothing about how he had sharpened the edge, though it wouldn't make the greatest weapon regardless of how sharp it was. It must not have been a pretty death.

"That a sail boat out there?" the Hammer said.

They looked toward the horizon at something too small to know what it was.

After a few moments the Hammer said, "Fuck that DNA police stuff. We're going where the Gestapo knows better than to interrupt a church service."

When they continued, Wendel remained a good distance behind the other two. An hour later they stopped to pick up some food for dinner at a grocery where the Hammer said, "Steaks are on me." While they watched the proprietor weigh the meat, the Hammer put his arm across Wendel's back and said, "You're easy to read, man. I know you were pissed about my breakfast contribution."

Even before the Hammer bought the steaks, Wendel decided he could co-exist with the guy despite his gratuitous remarks about the Gestapo, immigrants, gun control, and Ruby Ridge. Bottom line he wished they were meeting the Hammer in Idaho rather than traveling with him, but the trip would be okay.

Wendel pitched his tent while Brendan and the Hammer enjoyed a couple bottles of beer, teasing him about needing the tent. They enjoyed the woods without the shelter, and bragged about how many days they could survive without bringing along any food or water. He figured he was safe on the trip with Brendan along, but what if Brendan were the killer. Like the Hammer, Brendan had been around when both murders were committed, and certainly had the means. He hardly needed the tire iron. Yet using his hands would have directed attention at him, so of course if he were the killer, he would have made it look like someone else was guilty. Maybe Brendan and the Hammer were working together so that neither would worry about the other if one of them decided to kill Wendel.

Brendan had no motive for killing Handler—for that matter, the Hammer didn't either—except maybe to steal the painting. Neither knew Handler. Gorman's view of the world was not that different from the Hammer's, and the only statement even approaching politics Brendan had ever expressed was a Will Rogers quote that a comic didn't need a joke writer as long as the government was around.

Later in his sleeping bag Wendel thought about his bland life that had led him to take on this adventure. He could have left investigating the Hammer to the police, yet had chosen to make this trip. Somewhere in his genes was a risk taker making his debut.

He woke at six and walked to the campground lodge to fetch three coffees. Nothing threatening occurred on an easy day that took them across the state to Tahoe and then a hard day biking to beyond Boise. Three days in the saddle left Wendel's back aching and his still-sore leg even sorer.

At eight the third night Wendel called the Chief expecting he would be safely gone for the day.

"Yeah," said the familiar voice. "What do you want at this hour? Who's dead now?"

"You want me to call back?" Wendel said.

"Your murders are keeping me so busy I have to work nights just to do my paperwork and get my assistant paid."

"I'm up in Idaho for a week on my motorcycle. Just wanted to let you know I'm not on the run."

"If that tire iron is yours, I hope you won't need to change a tire," the Chief said.

"If you had shown me the one you found on Sunday, I could have told you whether it's mine. If it is someone stole it."

"Then his DNA will turn up."

Wendel wanted to say not necessarily, that he had used the iron after his motorcycle fall when his leg was bleeding, but he knew this sounded more like a lawyer's argument so he'd leave it to Demetrius Snyder. If someone were clever enough to murder Gorman with his tire iron, he'd be clever enough to leave Wendel's DNA and not his own. Maybe someone whose cheek was scraped Sunday, would turn up, but Wendel suspected if the killer were still a mystery to Wendel after his trip north, the Chief would arrest him soon after he returned.

"Just wanted to let you know I'm not hiding anything," he said to the Chief.

"More important, don't hide yourself. If we have to come after you we will."

On Friday the Hammer smelled the barn, refused to stop for lunch and pushed them on to Coeur d'Alene. "I want to make it before sundown," he said.

"We can ride tonight," Brendan said.

"Tonight's our Shabbat dinner," the Hammer said and rode off without responding to Brendan's "Huh?"

"I guess he's Jewish," Wendel said as Brendan passed him half a power bar. They buckled their helmets and followed.

As they drove, more and more turning aspens and cottonwoods greeted them. Wendel thought Idaho would be a good place to move to if so many intolerant people hadn't gotten there already.

The Hammer showed them around his simple though spacious log cabin in the woods north of Coeur d'Alene that abutted a mountainous national forest. They wouldn't be much more isolated if they were in the Himalayan Mountains. He could probably step outside and shake hands with a grizzly bear.

"Relax, enjoy yourselves, eat whatever's in the fridge and cupboards. Only place off limits is the basement, but don't worry. It's locked so you can't get down there anyway." Wendel pictured a subterranean art gallery with his Klee as the latest addition.

Wendel and Brendan would share a room with bunk beds, and Wendel gladly accepted the top. He had to walk through the Hammer's bedroom to use the only shower, mostly cold water because no one had stoked the Hammer's wood-burning water heater while he was away. On his way back through the bedroom Wendel saw a large pistol on the Hammer's nightstand. A 45, Brendan told him when Wendel mentioned it. "You don't want to get in front of it."

They climbed into the Hammer's '55 Chevy Bel Air to drive to the community center. "We're not Jewish," the Hammer said. "We respect the ancient Hebrews because they built their culture without a 'big-brother' telling them what to do."

"The Hebrews created the big brother," Brendan said.

"God's not the problem," the Hammer said.

"How about Moses?"

"Moses wasn't even Jewish. The Egyptian secret police did that burning bush trick and then installed him as Pharaoh's undercover agent when they knew the Hebrews were leaving. Once Moses came to power, he did what every tyrant does, betrayed Pharaoh, started his own regime, and when god kept him out of the promised land,

Moses put his brother, Aaron, in charge. The usual nepotism thing. The Ten-Commandment story is a biblical warning: even leaders with pure motives eventually usurp power. Now the government uses the commandments, which are nothing more than what people would do naturally if left alone. One more way to maintain control."

Nothing wrong with the Hammer's thinking, Wendel thought. Maybe these survivalists aren't so sinister, just a bunch of libertarians. The people they met at dinner made Wendel wonder even more, made him think for a moment he was back with the Brady Bunch. At one end of the hall that was about the size of a basketball court kids were playing blind-man's-bluff, while at the other end their parents were organizing a potluck. Several seniors sat in a semi-circle around a fireplace. Whatever the "congregation" might have done the rest of the week, they came together scrubbed, well mannered and with the kind of fellowship that made Wendel enjoy his own Sunday gospel-church service.

The three of them helped set up round tables and then, after loading their plates, sat with the Gershons, a family of four, including an adopted son, Joshua, who was the Hammer's godchild. The FBI had killed Joshua's parents in a raid when Joshua was 3 months old. The feds resisted the Hammer's attempt to adopt the child, claiming he wasn't fit, not only because of his manslaughter conviction and anti-social beliefs but also because he traveled too much, so the Hammer found a mom and pop, the Gershons, who would raise the boy. Papa Gershon delighted in telling how after the judge confirmed the adoption, the assistant US attorney stood up and claimed that the Attorney General objected.

"Fine, have the Attorney General in my courtroom at two this afternoon," the Judge said. Of course the AG didn't show up so the judge held the assistant in contempt and locked him up until the Attorney General sent someone from Washington to threaten federal reprisals against the state of Idaho.

One of the elders led a prayer that brought Wendel back to the reality. After thanking god for their food and their land, he said, "May god give us the sense and judgment to know when to obey the magistrates who are ordained for the peace, safety and good of the people and when it is our duty to disregard the magistrates because they act contrary to the word of god. May god give us the strength and power to resist an unholy government and rid this country of its scourge by force of arms if necessary."

On the ride back to the Hammer's cabin, Wendel said, "Sounds like you're ready for a revolution."

"If necessary to follow first principles," the Hammer said.

"What are first principles?" Wendel said.

"First principles are god's law," Brendan said.

"Thomas Jefferson wanted to update the constitution every twenty years if the judges failed to follow first principles," the Hammer said. "By revolution if necessary, at least until he became president."

"Let's talk about something more important," Brendan said. "Where are we biking tomorrow?"

The Hammer suggested some mountain trails, and Wendel thought about excuses to remain behind for an opportunity to search the Hammer's cabin.

21

A northern Idaho night in the low thirties tightened the lingering bruise in Wendel's leg. He recalled having, even without the injury, similar aches the previous winter when temperatures dipped near freezing. Was he getting old, or did he forget similar bumps and aches from his twenties and thirties? On the positive side, when he joined the others in the kitchen in response to the aroma of bacon, his limp gave credibility to his decision not to join them for the day.

At breakfast Wendel said, "What can I do around here or Coeur d'Alene if I give this leg a rest?"

The Hammer suggested walking around town if he was up to it, or a seaplane to fly over the lake and the area, or a spa with a hot tub and massage.

"They'll give you a pedicure if you're not careful," the Hammer said.

"Don't forget the mud bath and baby powder," Brendan said.

"Might as well wax your facial hair while you're at it," the Hammer said.

Wendel didn't mind the jokes. Getting a massage before he searched the Hammer's cabin felt like a good idea.

After breakfast, the Hammer dragged a backpack out of his front closet and removed a small knapsack. "The big one's my grab and go bag," he said.

"It's larger than I carried in the Navy," Brendan said. "What the hell have you got in there?"

"The small bag's for a day trip. The larger one I take when the government finds some excuse to declare martial law."

"I thought you lived off the land," Wendel said.

"If necessary, but this stuff helps. I've got knives, guns, poison darts, blowgun, potassium iodide for radiation, colloidal silver for an antibiotic, bleach for water, a compass, a GPS device, some rope, WD-40 oil. That's all in the small bag for when I have to travel light and can't take along the sleeping bag and tent, which are good to have in winter up here. I can live out there a long time with less."

"What do you use for warmth," Wendel asked.

"Caves or a fire if necessary. I can start a fire with a little magnifying glass, a battery, or gunpowder as a last straw."

Wendel wondered what was in the basement and what the Hammer did with it if he had to leave in a hurry, but he didn't ask. He probably blows the place up. They rode off together until Brendan and the Hammer veered onto a dirt road to meet some of the Hammer's friends for a ride in the Bitterroot Range in Eastern Idaho.

Wendel went to town for the massage. He should have plenty of time since the others had to ride an hour before they even started on the mountain trails. At the spa he forked over a couple hundred dollars for a sauna followed by a jump into the fifty-degree lake, a hot tub soak and then a massage. The routine left him with a serotonin surge that that did little to cure his soar leg.

On the ride back to the cabin, he pondered how much of a search he needed to satisfy Zvolens, and what were his chances of finding something that would save him from the fact that his tire iron was probably Gorman's murder weapon. He began by going through the Hammer's drawers, looking for a key to the basement and whatever else might turn up. Recalling some TV spy program while he was growing up, he wondered if the Hammer might have left a hair that opening a drawer would remove and give away his search. He didn't have the time or patience to look for hairs in every door and drawer he opened, so he shoved the concern out of his mind.

The Hammer's gun on the night table inspired great care going through the table's drawer. The drawer contained paper, pens, safety clips and other junk plus rubbers and a vibrator, but no key. A search of every drawer, cupboard, cabinet and closet in the cabin yielded nothing. Wendel did notice the non-descript art on the walls, mostly rural landscapes, one with British and American armies fighting during the revolution and a couple Thomas Kinkades. Not likely that the Hammer would want the Klee for this collection. If he stole it, he had probably already passed it along.

Frustrated, he boiled some water, brewed some tea and for a break stretched out in a tattered lounge chair on the porch. Laying back brought his gaze onto the eaves, which was where he kept his keys for when he locked himself out of his house. After a few minute's rest, he got up and searched under the eaves all around the house with no luck. He did stumble upon a ground-level window, no more than a foot high, which he guessed looked in on the basement. With his nose and one eye against the glass, he saw nothing inside a dark room, if in fact it was a room. Nor did the flashlight from his saddlebag allow him to see in.

While his effort ought to satisfy Zvolens, it had yielded nothing to take back to the Chief to hang the murder on the Hammer. When he returned to the porch chair, the St. Francis statue sitting out in the yard pissed him off—the thought that the peaceful saint reflected the Hammer's attitudes and basement arsenal or whatever the hell was down there. The statue inspired him to look in the Bible he had seen earlier with the idea that a key might be taped inside. Maybe the Hammer had created a secret compartment by carving out pages like Wendel had done to hide firecrackers and Playboy centerfolds from his parents when he was a kid, things his parents wouldn't have given a damn about, but just the same he had no brother or sister to hide things from.

Most of the Hammer's books were about war, organized chronologically, beginning with the Iliad and ending with several science fiction cyber-war tales. He found no key in the Bible—the Hammer probably would consider defacing the book as sacrilegious—nor in any of the others he thumbed through before returning to the porch and then the yard. He stood next to St. Francis and looked back at the house to see if a different perspective revealed other places to search.

Almost unconsciously he reached into and felt around the bowl in the saint's lap. Leaves and twigs but no key. Under the debris was a wing bolt that attached the bowl to the statue. With no other ideas, he unscrewed the bowl. Bonanza. Keys on a ring in St. Francis's lap.

The short run to the house reminded him of the soar leg. The third key he tried opened the basement door revealing a stairway that went down to a corridor and two locked doors. The same key opened the first and Wendel walked into the arsenal he had expected he'd find.

The image that struck him in barely serviceable light from the window was a long row of rifles standing on their butt-ends. A light switch next to the door lit the modest room, maybe twenty feet wide and thirty long, and showed that a bolted iron bar locked the rifles in the rack. Against the wall with the door were several laundry-like bins stuffed with ammo plus one with a stack of hand grenades. Wendel couldn't imagine how this discovery might help clear him of Gorman's murder.

"Find what you're looking for?" Rising suddenly over the grenade bin, Wendel hit his head on a shelf. The Hammer stood in the doorway, pointing a pistol at him. Fear seized him, greater than when he ran into the cougar in the mountains. Terror gripped the back of his neck and ran a chill down his body. He was going to die. Maybe right then, maybe later. Didn't matter. This was his last day on earth. Last day anywhere, he thought.

"Curiosity got the better of him," the Hammer said over his shoulder. "Like Orpheus?" The Hammer moved into the room and Gershon followed, a big smile on his face revealing his gold front tooth.

"I only—" Wendel started to say.

"You know who Orpheus was, don't you?"

"Not really."

"Tell him who Orpheus was, Gersh."

"Hades let Orpheus retrieve Eurydice from the underworld so long as Orpheus didn't look back until he was up in the living world. Guess what Orpheus did."

"Look back." Wendel said even though he knew he was participating in his own execution ritual.

"Orpheus did what he was told not to, just like you," the Hammer said. He not only lost Eurydice, but he pissed off his other female admirers so much that they ripped him apart. Sent him back to Hades in pieces. But I don't suspect you have female admirers."

"I was admiring your St. Francis when I saw the keys. I guessed you had some kind of arsenal in here, and yes, I was curious."

"Now you're fibbing," the Hammer said, "unless you unscrewed the bowl to admire the Saint's crotch." He and Gershon laughed.

"More like an outright lie than a fib," Gershon said. The Hammer motioned with the gun for Wendel to move away from the grenades. "You're here with your friend, Brendan, looking for evidence that I killed your neighbor, Gorman. Here's your evidence. I killed him. He welshed on a deal to deliver us some automatic rifles. We don't tolerate someone who breaks his word. Or who lies."

Wendel struggled for ideas to save his life. Where the hell was Brendan and how did the Hammer know that Wendel had talked with Brendan about searching the Hammer's place? If he could stay alive until Brendan returned, he'd have a chance.

"The others, by the way, are looking for me in the Bitterroot Range. We're playing cat and mouse. See if they can track me. Brendan could track me, but my friends are taking care of him. They don't like government agents. We've been onto him for months, trying to infiltrate our group."

Brendan a government agent. Of course. It explained his interest in The Hammer. The grip to the back of Wendel's neck tightened, like a cat with his hackles raised. His heart beat as though he had just run a mile.

"Your buddy's probably dead by now, so it's your turn."

The Hammer gestured to Gershon and the two of them grabbed Wendel's arms and pushed him out the door and up the stairs. Gershon pulled out a knife and pointed it toward the door. On the way he poked the tip into the small of Wendel's back.

"Where to?" Gershon said.

"Into the woods where the bears will have him for supper before anyone finds him."

"Bears don't like me," Wendel said.

"What do you mean?"

"I've run into three bears in my life and they all turned and ran."

"Scared them off did you."

"One was a grizzly." He'd given up on saving his life so why not be Wendel and bait these bastards. Better than shitting in his pants.

"Good story. Think your dead carcass will scare off an Idaho grizzly?"

They walked in silence. Every few steps Wendel felt the knifepoint. Dead leaves from previous years crunched under their shoes. A bird, one of the jays, announced their progress. Once Wendel stumbled and fell to the ground where several years of fallen leaves smelled of decay. Gershon grabbed his jacket and pulled him up with the knife at his throat, but the Hammer said, "No. We need to go further." As they walked on Wendel tried to breathe deeply, feel the magnificence of the woods as he never had. The Hammer finally stopped and nodded to Gershon.

"What will you tell the Gestapo when I don't show up next week?"

"Why should I tell him anything?"

"I phoned him the other night, told him the tire iron was mine and I'd be back from Idaho next week with answers that proved that you and not I killed Gorman."

"Sure, and he let you go rather than arrest you on the spot."

"I called him from southern Idaho. He couldn't stop me."

"Wait," the Hammer said to Gershon.

They stood in the forest where the animals and birds were now quiet spectators. Wendel wondered if animals sensed when one of their own was about to die. Supposedly humans were the only animals who lived with the knowledge that they would die, probably the reason humans invented religions. But maybe other animals sensed death in a nonverbal way like they sensed the coming of winter.

The Hammer took out his phone, waited to see if he had coverage and punched in a number. "We got Wendel," he said. After a moment he said, "Good. What do you plan to do with him?...Why don't you arrange a rock climbing accident, like a hundred foot fall. Be sure only one of you is the witness so you don't have to worry about conflicting stories. Just remember you went off today without Gersh and me."

Off the phone, the Hammer said, "We're going back," and he grabbed Wendel's arm. "I need more time to figure this out."

They pushed him back to the cabin where the Hammer retrieved some rope from his backpack.

"Lie down on your belly," the Hammer said. He pulled Wendel's arms behind him, crossed them at the wrists and then Gershon tied them together. Next they tied his legs.

"What now?" Gershon said.

"Wendel's going to have a motor cycle accident."

"With my hands tied behind my back?"

"Don't worry. You're in a holding pattern."

"Two guests dead the same day. That'll be convincing," Wendel said.

"I'd rather you commit suicide. Think about composing a suicide note. If it's believable, we'll give you a painless suicide. If not, it'll be slow and torture."

"I flunked creative writing," Wendel said. He'd rather make them work at figuring out his accident. Maybe give him a chance to work on getting away.

"Gersh, we need to put Wendel's bike in your truck and find the right place. Then we'll come back for him."

"Is he safe here?" Gershon interrupted cleaning his fingernails long enough to point his knife at Wendel.

"The basement will hold him."

They pushed him toward the stairs where Wendel used the wall and railing for support to hop a step at a time. Half way down the Hammer pushed him, and even though the banister broke part of the fall, Wendel's head cracked against the concrete steps. Next he knew he was laying on his back in front of the gun rack with Gershon and the Hammer standing over him. He tasted blood and his tongue felt a split in his lip.

"Why not put me in that other room," Wendel said. "These guns make me nervous."

"This will do, wise guy."

"The other room. Is that where you keep your art collection and my painting?"

"I don't have your painting, Wendel. Art's for city folk. The woods are my art."

"Sure," Wendel said. "And you didn't kill Handler."

"You're right there. You're the perfect setup for both murders. You have a connection with both. Not me. I didn't kill him. You never should have told me you killed Gorman, because that explains why I tied you up until I could call the police. Unfortunately you get away before the police come and have an accident. Let's go, Gersh."

The Hammer locked the door, leaving Wendel alone on the floor.

22

Wendel sat up with his back against the rifles, wondering how he could write a suicide note that would satisfy the Hammer and still tip off the police. The thought pissed him off. God damn it, he wouldn't cooperate. He'd rather have a painful accident. Cheryl had once told him that most pain was mental, and could by overcome with relaxation and meditation. He doubted it. Thoughts of never seeing Cheryl again added to the pain.

The acrid smell of gunpowder, which seemed to have seeped into the concrete-block walls, reminded him of Viet Nam. He felt like kicking his legs in rage, but the closeness of the wall discouraged him. He shifted back against the rifles for support, but instead the rack slid away. Using a rifle for leverage, he pulled himself up and thrust a shoulder into the row of rifles whose muzzles were several inches apart. They rattled in their slots and against the bar that held them locked in place.

When the entire rack tilted momentarily against the wall, he figured he could push it against the door and block the Hammer when he returned. But the door opened out so it would take about a nanosecond for the Hammer to figure it all out. He tried to hop toward the door but with his feet so close together, he lost his balance and fell onto the concrete, landing on his injured thigh. Using the rifles again he got up and waddled to the door. A push with his shoulder told him he had no chance of busting the thick panels.

He half-hopped, half-hobbled to the hand grenade bin. Straining his shoulders, he was able to raise his arms behind his back high enough to reach over the edge of the bin and then lower his hands to the grenades. Maybe one of these babies would blow out the door. He had never thrown one in combat, but the feel in his hand reminded him of how in basic training they had learned to use them. Pulling out the pin freed a lever that would spring out and trigger the fuse once he released the lever by heaving the grenade over a reinforced wall. His sergeant stood beside him ready to save him and the rest of the squad in case he dropped the grenade or klutzed it into rather than over the wall.

Memory of the army lecture on grenades offered other problems. Some were percussion grenades, designed for the energy waves to blow out the enemies' brains in a confined space. At least he'd go in a hurry, and besides he couldn't see how percussion grenades could help the Hammer in his war against a future American dictator. Other grenades were so powerful their explosion would leave Wendel deaf. Maybe the explosion would blow out the tiny window and dissipate some of the deafening roar, but if not, better deaf than dead. What he hoped was that the grenades were the type designed not so much to kill the enemy as to inflict as many wounds as possible with small fragments of shrapnel. The wounded would require the attention of others and allow the launcher more opportunity to counter-attack or escape. This third kind of grenade made the most sense for a future Hammer-like guerrilla war.

He looked for a place to shelter himself when a grenade went off in the room. He hopped to the door, this time without falling, pretended to drop the grenade and hopped to the other end of the room. One, two, three, he counted, and made it a second ahead of the four-second fuse even though he stumbled and almost fell. Were the fuses still four seconds, he wondered. Moreover there was nothing to protect him. The shrapnel would shred him anywhere in the room. He might only lose an arm, a leg and half his head. The Hammer would tell the police that Wendel broke into the room and had an accident.

He hopped to the rifle rack where he used first his hands and then his shoulder to angle an end of the rack out from the wall. Back at the door, he pretended to drop the grenade and hopped back to and around the rifles, falling to the floor somewhere between the counts of three and four. The metal slab that held the rifles in place was a foot high and offered some protection. Above the slab, the rifle stocks were about two or three inches apart and might help. Was the wood strong enough to protect him from the shrapnel or were the rifles more like a mobile home in a tornado. He didn't have much choice. The canvas grenade bin with spindly metal legs was no protection, and besides he didn't like the idea of hiding behind a pile of grenades. That thought made him realize that the explosion might set off other grenades, but again he had no options and guessed that the grenades were not that unstable.

He moved again to the door, aware that he was getting pretty good at hopping, regardless of how unsteady he felt. Behind his back he eased out the pin a couple centimeters. With a firm grip on the lever, he pulled the pin all the way out and dropped it to the floor. At that moment he thought about how this was a stupid thing to do. He considered the alternatives and without a second thought, dropped the grenade.

Hop, hop. One, two, three, four hops. When he reached the fifth, he knew he hopped faster than one per second. After the sixth hop he thrust himself forward onto the floor behind the rifles.

The explosion pounded his ears. He might be deaf but was alive, inhaling smoke and dust and probably sawdust and concrete. A dense odor made him gag. The first thing he saw was blood on the floor next to his head. His legs and arms behind his back felt on fire, and he rolled over to quench any flame. The burns didn't go away but he was pretty sure they were from wounds and not ongoing fire. Probably ricocheted shrapnel had seared his pants and fleece jacket. Slowly he pulled himself up and best he could checked the front of his body. His leg ached from the earlier fall. Then he saw that the grenade had destroyed most of the door. He could get out.

Making it upstairs was another story. He couldn't jump high enough to reach a step. With help from the railing, he sat and one at time pushed himself backwards up the stairs. He had to get rid of the ropes or he wasn't going anywhere.

On his first hop toward the kitchen his tired legs collapsed. He crawled and then used his teeth on the knob to pull out a drawer. Dish towels wouldn't help. Nor would silverware in the next drawer. The third held the knives. His legs held when he stood and behind his back, he grasped a serrated knife. Quickly he surveyed the room and chose the back door as a wedge. On the porch, he nudged the door to almost closed, and put the knife in the opening. Before he could secure it by leaning against the door, it fell to the porch, almost between the wood slats, but not quite. He sat, leaned back and retrieved it. The second time worked. The door held the knife while he worked his hands back and forth. Not like slicing tomatoes, but it did the job.

Cutting the rope on his legs was a snap. He had burns on his arms and legs and a minor wound just above his wrist. The rifle rack had protected him. He limped through the house toward the front door where he noticed the Hammer's grab and go bag. Quickly he rummaged and snatched some bandages and antibiotic cream. Outside he realized his hearing wasn't totally gone when he heard a motorcycle, still a ways down the road but coming his way. He turned and ran the opposite direction into the woods.

23

He ran and ran. When his lungs or legs screamed, he slowed to a fast limp. After at least an hour, he paused and bandaged his wounds. Leaning against a tree, he realized he had made a bad mistake. He should have gone sideways from the road and then out to the main road after the motorcycle passed him toward the house. Instead he had run into the immense national forest where he had no experience or abilities and where the Hammer was totally at home. The Hammer would track him, quickly if he had a dog, but probably almost as quickly without. The Hammer would enjoy hunting him down in his favorite environment. He'd come with a gun or maybe his blowgun and poison darts. Wendel sank into a funk.

When his mind stopped abusing him, he began to think. He was a city guy, used to taming computers with the logical part of his brain. Thinking ability gave him one advantage over the Hammer, not a great advantage in the forest, but the only one he had. He needed to find a place where he could surprise the Hammer, where he'd have a chance before the Hammer could shoot him. And he needed a weapon because the Hammer would certainly get the better of him if he had none. The Hammer might be overconfident, another advantage.

He realized the forest had changed, grown darker. He had lost his watch and his sense of time, but it was obvious he needed to prepare for a night in the woods without a tent, sleeping bag or blankets. Early October temperatures in Northern Idaho would probably sink below freezing.

More slowly he walked trying to angle ninety degrees away from the route he had been following. The next day he'd circle back to find the road. Aches and pains called out all over his body, the burns, the old bruise in his leg, and twinges whose origins he couldn't recall. Before it was totally dark he came to a large boulder. On what he thought was the south side he scooped leaves and dirt away until enough of a hole existed to let him lay partially under ground level. He applied the antibiotic cream and fashioned an amateur's bandage before lying down in the cavity. He tried to cover his body with the loose leaves and dirt as best he could. He smelled the gunpowder on his fleece jacket, wished he could get rid of the odor but couldn't. The previous autumn's leaves covered him enough to immerse him in the aroma of a rotting forest.

Next he knew he had just awakened and had no idea how long he had slept. It was dark, no visible moon; he saw or sensed the silhouettes of trees. Dirt had gotten into his mouth and dried it out. He hadn't had water since the morning before. The forest was still except for the hoot of an owl. No matter how adept was the Hammer, he couldn't sneak up in this stillness without Wendel being aware. He thought about getting up and moving on, but then he'd make noise that would alert a nearby Hammer, so he waited. Waiting made him realize he was cold. Was he cold enough to get hyperthermia or hypothermia? He couldn't keep them straight.

If he slept any more, he wasn't aware. Once he heard an animal tramping in the distance. The noise—he imagined a bear—came nearer but then passed by. Could the Hammer hear his shivers against the leaves? With the early glimmers of light, the forest came to life. Birds sang and called, small animals darted through the leaves. When there was enough light and noise that he could make his way without sounding like an ox, he got up. Out of habit or intuition of not leaving an obvious trail, he "made" his bed, scooping dirt and leaves to re-cover the hole.

It took a couple of minutes to reorient off the boulder he'd slept next to toward the route he wanted to take—sideways for a mile or so and then hopefully back the way he came. He found a couple rocks for the unlikely event that he got into hand-to-hand combat with the Hammer. Slowly he made his way. He had all day to get out of these woods, which he ought to be able to do even at a moderate pace that allowed him to listen for another human being. He hadn't walked far before he realized he was thirsty and hungry. Silently he thanked the Hammer for yesterday's bacon and eggs.

When he paused to rest after an hour, his bruises and burns hurt all at once. Then he heard the nearby sound of an animal or person. He listened for more. One bird sang but the rest had ended their morning symphony. He heard it again. Then: "Yes, Wendel. It's me."

Frantically he searched in the direction of the voice, then shifted behind a tree.

"I hand it to you getting out of my basement, but this is as far as you go."

Fight and flight tore at him. He didn't answer.

"I'm ten years younger than you, in better shape, and I know my way around. I'm looking forward to the hunt."

Wendel hardly heard because he was already running.

24

Wendel sprinted, then slowed when he couldn't maintain the pace, finally stopped behind a tree. No need to test the pulse in his neck to feel it race. Sweat ran into his eyes. When he looked back a dart twanged into the trunk. On he went, trying to keep trees between himself and the Hammer. Maybe toward the main road. Why the hell were there no paths. Didn't anyone hike in these woods? Another dart each time he adjusted his route. Was the Hammer herding him? Where?

He stopped for a breath. The Hammer, younger, faster, could have caught Wendel by now. But the Hammer didn't want to poison him with a dart. He wanted Wendel to have an accident, not as good as suicide, but an accident worked for the Hammer.

So he slowed to a fast walk. Save his energy for when the Hammer decided it was time for the accident. One of the rocks had slipped out of his hand but he had the other. After the next dart he turned and threw the rock in the Hammer's direction.

"Good, Wendel. Fight back."

"Where are you herding me?" Weird, he thought, having a conversation with a guy trying to kill me.

"There's a little obstacle course up ahead. Get through it and you live."

Wendel turned at a right angle, and The Hammer responded with a dart. "Go that way and I'll have to kill you."

Wendel turned back toward the obstacle course. At least he knew the way out, the direction the Hammer didn't want him to take. He walked slowly enough to register the spicy aroma of the young cedars he was climbing through. He grabbed a stick to help him along. What kind of obstacle course could the Hammer have built in the middle of the forest? Training for him and his fellow survivalists? How could he plan? He didn't know what kind of course. The rise became steeper. His neck pulse returned. Up ahead a woodpecker mocked him with its call.

"You're almost there," the Hammer called.

"There" hardly looked like an obstacle course. Up ahead loomed a cliff and as Wendel came closer he saw his choices—climb almost straight down about 300 feet or walk across a 30- or 40-foot-wide rock ledge. One border of the ledge was the face of the cliff, perhaps too steep for even professional rock climbers. The other border was the same 300-foot drop, straight down. The perfect accident. He could hear the Hammer: "We had a great hike, but then Wendel slipped. I tried to grab him but couldn't."

Wendel put one foot onto the ledge. It sloped gradually toward the fall but not so steep that he couldn't walk. Or so it seemed. When he started, he stepped on finely-ground rock, slippery as hell. Could he take even a step without his feet sliding out from under him toward the edge? He could but only by leaning out in the direction of the fall.

"You're doing great. Keep going," called the Hammer.

The stick was little help—it slipped each time he tried to plant it. Wendel quickly learned not to stand up straight or lean toward the cliff wall, which made his feet start to slide. Twice he almost skidded onto his back and surely would have slid off. He had to remain leaning toward the edge to stay on his feet. Leaning forward, toward the edge drove his feet into the granite rather than out from under him. The stick helped him balance. Ahead the surface was covered with denser rock, almost powder that was flaking off the cliff wall. He doubted he could stay upright even if he leaned outward.

If he could make another thirty feet or so, the cliff wall bent gradually so that the curve might protect him from the Hammer's darts. Slowly he stepped and shuffled. His feet did slide but again he caught himself by leaning out farther. Could he possibly make it all the way across? If so, he'd have a temporary advantage because the Hammer couldn't pursue him as fast as Wendel could run. Yet he didn't know where he'd run.

Five steps further revealed a bleak reality. The ledge tapered down to several feet and then disappeared. There was no way across.

Right here he'd have to take on the Hammer. He turned back and planted his feet as firmly as he could. A crag gave him an inadequate grip of the cliff wall, but it was better than none. He waited. And waited. Moments passed until he realized the Hammer didn't need to walk out. He could just wait for Wendel to fall or walk back.

"Come and get me Hammer," he challenged. "You want to fight me out here or back there where there's more room?"

Silence.

"I'm writing a note to stick in my pocket, explaining that you killed Gorman, your arsenal, and why I fell off this cliff. You better come get this note or you're cooked.

After a moment the Hammer called out, "On my way."

Wendel waited. He could see enough around the gradual curve that he'd have at least some warning that the Hammer was about to arrive. He slipped off the fleece jacket. It fell toward the ledge but he caught it, ran the stick through a sleeve, and gripped the end of the stick and sleeve. The Hammer's footsteps and short slides in the loose rock came nearer.

When the Hammer drew close, Wendel got ready. With the Hammer within reach, Wendel swung out his arm. Instinctively the Hammer reached up to grab the fleece, but all he got was the end of the other sleeve. The sudden movement without something of substance to grab made him lose balance and his feet started to slide out from under him. He leaned precariously toward the edge, trying to dig his heels for traction, but without success. His slide stopped only when the fleece became taut. Wendel held the other end with one hand and the crag with the finger tips of his other hand.

"Help me Wendel. Pull me back and we'll both walk out of here. You'll never find your way alone."

Wendel waited, for a moment unsure if he could believe the Hammer, or even if he couldn't, whether he'd be hopelessly lost without the man. Then he said," Pull yourself up."

The Hammer began to right himself with the leverage of the taut fleece. When he was halfway upright, Wendel let go. The stick, the fleece and the Hammer fell 300 feet, his last words—"son of..."—growing inaudible as he sailed away. Relief spread through Wendel, for a moment causing him to relax his grip on the crag, but he caught himself and sank back against the wall.

Instant fatigue seduced him to rest where he was, but he had to get off the cliff and out of the woods or he'd be as dead as the Hammer. After a few minutes he carefully retraced his way back over the ledge to where he had begun. Waiting for him when he got there was the Hammer's knapsack. The sack contained a half-full canteen, and Wendel contained himself to drink only a couple swallows. He'd need some later. The pack also had half an energy bar, and Wendel devoured half of what was left.

He was shaking, so he sat down to recover. As the shakes gave way, elation spread over his body. He had beaten a man trained to survive on his wits in the woods and saved his own life. He, Wendel, the nerd. It was hardly believable.

The woods were quiet, perhaps in response to the violence, perhaps for the midday. After a few minutes Wendel crawled toward the edge of the cliff and carefully looked over. He wanted to see the dead body, but the Hammer had fallen around the curve and wasn't visible. The realization that he had killed a man, even a bad man, grabbed his gut. He lay there trying to reconcile the feeling with his lack of remorse. He couldn't, at least not now, when he had to get out of the forest.

He retraced the way down the climb until he reached about the point where the Hammer had told him not to turn. Then he headed in the forbidden direction. The woods seemed livelier, some animals and birds making their sounds. Another bite of the bar tasted almost as good as the first as did some water. Though he had been heartened at first, after a few hours he thought he might be walking in circles or maybe further into the national forest. He also figured he had to be careful of stumbling upon Gershon or other compatriots of the Hammer.

Without any warning, he heard a voice say, "Wendel." Startled he moved behind a tree. "It's me, Brendan." Sure enough he recognized the voice.

"They said they were going to kill you."

"Not much chance of four guys getting the better of me in the woods."

Brendan had a story to tell but not before they got out of the forest. Brendan knew the way.

Wendel wanted to go home but couldn't. Federal agents commandeered the Hammer's cabin. They wanted Wendel's story. The old Wendel, alive and well, told an agent to go fuck himself. He'd tell them nothing until he found a bathroom, a shower and dinner. Brendan restrained the agent, said he'd keep an eye on Wendel and then drove the two of them to a motel in Coeur d'Alene.

The next day he learned the Feds had taken Gershon into custody and obtained a confession. The Hammer and Gershon had run a stolen truck over his motorcycle on a back road. They returned to fetch him to leave him dead at the "accident." Dealing with the Feds and then his insurance company left him longing for his bungalow on the beach and the calmer, if not simpler, task of nursing the GeTechNome project.

At first the Feds wouldn't tell him what was in the other locked basement room, even after he told them of the earlier murder of Handler at his home and his missing painting. They assured him that the room did not contain an art collection. Brendan told him confidentially that the Hammer was using the room to build bombs. The room contained explosive hardware and other bomb-making equipment, like the kind used by a survivalist back when Atlanta hosted the Olympic games.

Brendan explained that three weeks ago when he had met the Chief, Brendan and the Chief had together called his contact at the Justice Department to vouch for Brendan.

"I figured I'd protect you," Brendan said. "Turns out you're a stud as well as a hero and didn't need my help."

The next morning, Brendan drove him to the Spokane airport to catch an Alaskan Airlines flight to L.A. Wendel spent the flight thinking about how Brendan and the Chief had been using him to do their dirty work. He couldn't leave out Zvolens. To all these people, Wendel's safety was an afterthought. Now it was time for him to take care of himself. He wondered if Cheryl had returned home and looked forward to a soak in the hot tub.

25

The most intriguing message on Wendel's answering machine at home was from Margo. "I saw the news coverage from Idaho. Call as soon as possible. We want to make a movie."

"The story's not complete," he said when he reached her. "the police are looking for Handler's killer."

"We'll start while you're hot, all over the news, CNN, Fox, even the New York Times, breaking up a terrorist plot."

At first Wendel had loved the ego massage from giving the interviews. But after a day of aggressive reporters and camera crews he'd had enough, and then came the ego deflation as the media moved onto a new story about a politician whose mistress disclosed that he wore his wife's panties.

"We can make up a better ending than life," Margo said, interrupting his thoughts.

"Will you be playing yourself in the movie?"

"What do you mean?"

"The successful woman, suspect for killing her French lover."

"We'll leave that part out," she said with a laugh, maybe a nervous laugh.

"Hard to believe you stole the painting you hated. Do you think the killer stole the painting?"

"How I love that painting," Margo said. "It will be perfect on movie posters."

"Yeah, sure." Wendel recalled Margo insisting he not hang it in any room she had to come into. "Any word from your husband on his computer work? I need to make some money."

"The movie will make you a bundle and if you want to work on Howard's computers, we can arrange that too."

Wendel agreed to meet her at his house Friday morning to discuss the movie. Difficult to imagine Margo and himself as a quarreling young couple—now the woman who makes grownup movies and the man who conquered a terrorist cell. She didn't seem too concerned about being a suspect for Handler's murder.

Cheryl wasn't home so he left a message. That evening in the hot tub he told her about Idaho, and she surprised him with the news that she had gotten a job with one of the vineyards. She would be calling on wine shops in Southern California and arranging promotional tastings, which she would attend as the vineyard's rep. They climbed out of the tub and mellowed on the patio with a glass of the Chardonnay she was promoting, featuring a so-so twinge of oak.

Wendel raised his glass and said, "To the memory of our unconsummated honeymoon."

After Cheryl clinked his glass, he added, "And to the remedial action we're about to take."

They thrashed in the sheets, like teenagers, caught their breaths and then relished an hour or so in repeating cycles of pleasure and restraint until first she and then he burst with delight. As she dozed with her head on his chest, Cheryl's unique smell—garden-natural with a hint of rose—drew him even closer, a smell he could relish day after day. They began to arouse each other again, and with each caress Wendel released more tension from the dread of being hunted by the Hammer and then having killed a man. Afterwards they napped until the stillness of evening awakened him. For the first time since that day in the forest, he remembered the moment when the Hammer asked for help on the rock ledge and how he released the jacket allowing him to plunge to his death. Never in the past would he have thought he could appreciate the pleasure of killing a man that he felt right now, lying in bed.

Later Wendel returned to the hot tub to nurse his bruises, while Cheryl threw together a couple sandwiches and joined him with the bottle of wine. They lounged in the tub as a warm rain started to fall from the remnants of a hurricane that had wreaked havoc across the Baja. He knew the third glass would play havoc with his head the next day, but so what. Maybe the wine would ease the aches and pains.

"Now that we've fucked," Cheryl said, "we can get to know each other."

"Is that what you tell all your guys?"

"On my retreat I decided to give up all my guys. I'd like a deeper relationship with my hero."

A chill ran down Wendel's back, a mixture of excitement and fear. Despite the time they spent naked in the tub, their friendship, until recently, was neighborly only. Now they shared a trip to Europe, some banter, and an evening of lovemaking. He wondered if he was ready to share emotional intimacy. He groped for how to respond and came up with, "Maybe we ought to go on a retreat together."

"I have a surprise for you," she said.

"I love surprises. Fire away."

"Sunday night. Tomorrow I go on the road with a trainer and my wine. Saturday we have a tasting in Palm Springs."

"Give me a hint, please, please," he teased with the voice of a child.

"You'll like it."

Wendel looked forward with excitement but also felt relief to put off thoughts of commitment. Besides he had enough to do that he could wait for surprises, and if it was worth waiting for, he'd enjoy it even more. Meanwhile he had a movie to make, GeTechNome to put on line, hopefully Howard Taylor's conglomerate to sign up, and maybe even time to buy a new motorcycle with his insurance proceeds. For the night Cheryl and he cozied together while the storm beat against the roof. Rain was still pouring down when her alarm woke them at six. While she got ready for the day, he lay in bed, unable to get back to sleep, listening to Cheryl, the wind and the rain. With Cheryl's new hours, living next door to each other would be a blessing for their relationship.

He left the house at nine, grabbed a large coffee at Starbucks and walked over to the police station where the Chief sat with someone in his office.

"I came to pick up my computers," he said to Myrna, the assistant, as he sat down on a chair by her desk.

"The Chief didn't say anything about it, but he shouldn't be long."

Wendel saw his name upside down on the file Myrna was working on and asked, "What have you got on me."

"That you're a dangerous perp," the Chief said as he walked out of his office.

"You're welcome for solving one of your murders," Wendel said.

"Solved? Do we have anything to go on besides your word?"

"Like did I ask the Hammer to sign a confession before he tried to kill me?"

"Facts are you owned Gorman's murder weapon. The weapon gave you the means, you were in the area, and you had a motive. That's usually enough for a jury." The Chief stood over him, making Wendel feel like a defendant in the dock. Myrna was smiling at him, as though she pitied him. Didn't the damn file she was reading tell how he had thrown the Hammer off the cliff?

"So I have to bankrupt myself by hiring a lawyer?"

"Then you'd have to sell your house and I wouldn't have to put up with you any longer."

Wendel detected a slight smile on the Chief's face. It didn't last long, but he took a chance and said, "Losing me would ruin your life."

"Yeah, I'd have to retire."

"Without me a bright young woman like Myrna would get bored shuffling your parking tickets."

"What do you think, Myrna?" the Chief said. He was quiet, signaling it wasn't just a rhetorical question.

"The Hammer also had the means, was in the area, and had a motive," she said.

"You're doing your homework in the your criminal justice class," the Chief said. "Wendel, until I learn something new, you're a free man. But don't run off without telling me where you're going."

He walked out with both computers, a lot lighter than the weight of being on the wanted list. They had played with him, but that was okay, except that a beautiful young thing like Myrna ought to have more respect for a hero.

He spent the rest of the day at GeTechNome setting up the trial experiments that he and the willing scientists would work on from home. The research labs occupied a labyrinth of stately rooms. Waldo Peterson volunteered his lab for all the scientists to gather and watch the inauguration. "It probably won't work," Peterson said.

"If it does," Wendel said, "it will be the first time ever on a first try for one of my programs."

Actually he knew the computer would make the initial choice correctly because at the beginning there were no variables so he could rig the action. Sure enough the analog attachment delivered 8 ccs of the designated chemical into a flask. Simultaneously the wireless printer rattled out a message. They gathered around to read, "Fooled you. It can be done," which brought laughter and some hoots.

The next step wasn't so smooth as a different chemical tube emptied all its contents, overflowing the flask. One of the scientists sat at the keyboard and typed in, "Not so fast, Frankenstein," which the printer announced.

They worked past midnight until they were satisfied. Wendel helped the scientists set up equipment for their experiments and demonstrated the key-chain device that delivered ever-changing passwords. The guard let them out of the building, and Peterson and he walked to the parking lot together.

"Thanks for all your help," Wendel said. "You pushed me to do a better job."

"And you convinced me this might work," Peterson said. "I'll give it a try."

26

Friday morning Margo walked into the front hall followed by two women and a man, introduced as the screenwriter, the set designer and the greensman, or in this case, the greenswoman.

The four of them joked that "greensman" was the title for a position in the film industry so that's what they called the greenswoman.

"My job is to make the studio look like your yard," she said. "I put green trees and shrubs around the set."

"We usually don't bring this crew in this early," Margo said, "but we're fast-tracking while the story's fresh."

"Is this where you found the body?" the set designer said.

Wendel showed the location and explained the direction. The memory also brought back the odor from that night. Was it in the walls or just in his head? The orientation of the body—head closer than feet to the front door—made him realize for the first time that Handler had probably come home and surprised an intruder rather than the arriving murderer shooting Handler upon his opening the door.

After Wendel gave them an outline of his past two weeks, the screenwriter said, "We'll make you and the Navy Seal into one character."

"That ruins the story," Margo said. "The schlump kills the terrorist while the Seal is off playing. That's the story line."

Wendel of course agreed though he could do without the schlump characterization.

"Do you want a comedy or an action movie?" asked the screenwriter, casting a glance at Wendel when she said "comedy."

"Action. A hero with whom everyone can identify," Margo said.

"Are we casting Tom Cruise or Martin Short?"

"Tom Cruise of 'Risky Business' would be just fine."

The three movie people scoped out the house and backyard, tape measure, camera and sketchpad in hand, while Wendel made coffee. Through the window he watched the greensman, dressed more like a landscaper than a Home and Garden editor, flit around the yard with a flair of the master of the environment. When she examined some ferns that had overgrown their space, she squatted like his Japanese gardener with her butt almost reaching the ground between her feet.

"I'd miss you if you'd fallen off that mountain," Margo said as he set two mugs on the patio table.

"Who would have thought? I'd feel the same if it were you."

"Twenty years away from each other allowed us both to grow up."

"Grow up? Who says I needed to grow up?" he said with a smile.

"This is true. You've learned how to prosper while remaining immature."

Touche, he thought. When he considered having gone to Idaho, he had to agree.

"Your Chief of police called me while you were away," Margo said. "I'm still on his list of suspects."

Being awfully cool if she did it, Wendel thought. "Did you convince him you're innocent?"

"I doubt it. I didn't tell your Chief, but I knew the Handler tryst was a mistake right in the middle of my orgasm, "

"I'd like to watch the casting trials for that quality."

"You still like to provoke me," she said. "We'll leave the movie sex for your friend next door, what's her name."

The set designer sat down between them, interrupting Wendel's thoughts about the coming Sunday evening with Cheryl. "We can shoot most of the home shots here. We'll do the intimate shots, like in the bedroom, at the studio."

"Who are you going to stick the first murder on?" Wendel asked.

"You tell us."

He ran through the possibilities. When he mentioned Burgher, the screenwriter said he was too obvious. For the movie it will have to be someone else.

"The audience will think it's so obvious that it can't be him," Margo said. "So maybe it works for it to be him."

"How about multiple endings?" the screenwriter said. "Let the audience decide—they'll pay multiple times to vote. We'll double the take before we sell the overseas rights."

Movie people are like a software developer with an idea, Wendel thought, counting their billion-dollar sales and academy awards before shooting a single scene.

The screenwriter asked to see the emails and Wendel realized he hadn't looked at either computer since he'd reclaimed them. Would the Feds have altered or removed anything?

As he led them upstairs to this office, they looked out the back toward the dunes and the ocean. He thought how lucky he was to have this house, and even though Margo hadn't discussed money, he was likely to have a pretty good payday on the movie. Now that GeTechNome was into tests, they'd have a hard time not paying him if they got nervous about security and dropped the project. His money problems ought to be over for a while.

Handler's email files Wendel had saved looked in tack on his older computer, and he quickly found the email to Burgher sending the picture of the Klee.

"Fabulous," the screenwriter said. "Marketing will love it. 'The Death Painting' or something like that will turn them on."

Wendel reread the brief message: "Jacob, Attached is a photo of what appears to be a Klee print. I've never seen this Klee and wonder if you have and if you know who owns the original."

"Is this email from you or from Handler?" the screenwriter said. "It's on your computer."

"My computer but sent by Handler on let's see, September 4th, while I was in France and he was staying here."

Looking again at the email made Wendel realize the "Jacob" was too informal for Handler who hardly knew Burgher. Wendel scrolled back to see if he had missed a previous contact when he looked on the day after he got home from France. He found several art business emails, two more from Handler to Ginette and nothing more.

"How about the message back from the Swiss guy? About the painting being a fake," Margo said.

Wendel found the most recent email, from Ginette, perhaps received on the day Handler was shot. Scrolling backwards he found no return message from Burgher. For a moment he thought it had disappeared, but then he recalled finding the email when he was at GeTechNome and finding it on the Entwurf's domain rather than his own inbox. Burgher might have emailed to Wendel's computer, but if so, it was never delivered. Suddenly it struck him. Burgher must have sent that email to a different address, maybe to the killer.

Wendel shared his thinking with the screenwriter and Margo, carefully watching Margo for a reaction. He was almost certain she hadn't photographed the Klee she hated. Handler had told her it was worth millions of dollars, but she thought he was talking about the original, not a three-dollar copy. Margo looked alert and interested but not concerned that the killer's identity was sitting on Burgher's computer that Wendel had already hacked into once.

The set designer and greensman had walked up behind them and had heard part of the conversation. The set designer said, "Why not hack in again?"

"In front of all these witnesses?" Wendel said.

"Our lips are sealed," Margo said.

"Except for in the movie," the screenwriter said.

Wendel made a half-hearted attempt. He didn't want all these people in on the discovery if he were successful. Why he wasn't sure, but suspected his desire for secrecy had something to do with being in control. He also was in no hurry, kind of like a lion that had stalked its prey, but was content to leisurely enjoy the catch. He wanted to get Margo and the movie people out of the house and then attack the Entwurf. He told them the Entwurf must have increased its security, that he needed some additional software he'd have to update from his other computer and on line, which would take some time.

"Maybe the email back from Burgher is on your other computer," the screenwriter said.

"I had it on vacation in Europe and never received anything on Klee."

"Before we leave, I'd like to meet your neighbor," the screenwriter said.

"And show us the bomb shelter," Margo said and explained the shelter to the others. "We have to find some way to use it in the movie."

"We also need to figure out what we film in Idaho," said the screenwriter.

Wendel told them they could go to Idaho without him, but that he'd be delighted to let them know when Cheryl was back in town. The yard had that fresh feel that follows a storm. They were fortunate that the vestiges of the hurricane had ended the wild fire season, which added to the sense of wellbeing he'd felt all day and would enjoy even more if he could nail the other killer.

Inside the bomb shelter the floor was damp. Underground water must have seeped through during the storm surge, and even though the walls had deteriorated, this was the first time water had invaded. He had lived on the changing coast long enough to know the ocean would eventually not only overwhelm the shelter but would take back his home. Sometimes he felt like he had a ninety-nine year lease, so that if an earthquake didn't end his occupancy, the property would drop into the surf sometime short of 2100. He made a mental note (whatever those were worth as he moved through middle age) to call one of his vineyard acquaintances to see if the dampness was bad for the wine. Or Cheryl could get that answer from her employer.

The set designer whistled and said, "This place is great. Quirky. We'll hang some gas masks on the wall and maybe add some old guns. My mom told me that in the sixties people with shelters kept guns to keep out the neighbors after an attack, to horde the food and water. We can hang a picture of JFK and add some other stuff."

Finally they left. He was relieved and turned down Margo's offer to talk money. Probably smart to wait until the studio had more time and dollars invested.

While his computer came back to life, he called for a pizza and a salad. Who the hell had Burgher sent that email to announcing that the Klee was a fake? Whoever it was, had Burgher told him (or was it a her) he wanted to spend five million to buy the fake. Had Burgher brought him (or her) into his plan to fly to LA.

The Entwurf's security blocked his first approach. He backed off and entered the GeTechNome computer system where he retrieved his own software used to break codes. Domesticating the code-breaking software on his older laptop presented problems because the operating system wasn't compatible.

Using his new computer and the software from GeTechNome, he had no trouble probing the Entwurf's system and finding Burgher's email files. He "thumbed" through the inbox until he found the first email from Handler, or rather the killer, that had been sent on Wendel's old laptop. Again the familiar tone of the unsigned email suggested that Handler, who probably didn't know Burgher, had not sent the email. Next he switched to Burgher's outbox and scrolled forward from September 4.

Burgher sent lots of emails in English, and despite Wendel's anticipation to know who the killer was, his curiosity grabbed hold to see what kind of messages Burgher sent. The art world described them all. Business communications like inquiries about paintings and auctions, answers to queries about the Foundation, just what Wendel would expect from a legitimate Entwurf. Slowing to read these messages reminded him of Christmas when he was as a kid and had delayed getting to the big present, the one he'd written to Santa about, while first opening the socks from Aunt Dorothea or the book from Uncle Albert.

The discovery in Burgher's outbox, the email he had read four weeks ago at GeTechNome, could have booted him right out of his chair. The message saying the Klee was a fake was from Burgher to Cheryl.

27

He got up and paced the room, noting and then ignoring the beautiful day on the ocean. Had Cheryl murdered Handler? Why? Their trip to Switzerland a charade between Burgher and Cheryl? He, Wendel, duped? Out the window over the hedge he spied a corner of Cheryl's hot tub where he and she had discussed the murder while they soaked. How in the hell did Burgher even know Cheryl's email address?

She came in and out of his house regularly, she had a key or came off the patio where he seldom locked the door. She might even have sent an email from her own computer for Handler with whom she'd shared her hot tub. But...a big but, why the familiar tone in Burgher's email back to Cheryl, as though they knew each other, which made the trip to Lucerne a show.

Wendel couldn't sleep, anxious about Cheryl's role in Handler's murder and the stolen painting. About four he fell off until daylight woke him in a funk, all the more because Idaho and then his night with Cheryl had created an illusion of a new charmed life. He thought about calling Cheryl but didn't have her cell phone number, a reminder of the novelty of their romance.

In the village he bought three coffees and shared them with the Chief and Myrna. He didn't tell the Chief about his computer hacking of the day before, better to understand the terrain before sharing it.

"We have nothing new on Burgher," the Chief said.

"Maybe I'll hack into his computer system."

"What you're able to do on a computer alarms me more than Burgher right now."

"The FBI does it all the time," Wendel said.

"What gives you that idea?"

"You know better than I, having collaborated with them."

"The FBI isn't as competent as you seem to be. You ought to get a job helping them out. By the way the DNA tests came back. You're all over Gorman's murder weapon."

"Surprise. What else did you expect?" Wendel couldn't hide his impatience, tired of being a suspect, manipulated into chasing after Burgher and the Hammer to clear himself. What did the Chief want now?

"No match for your Idaho buddy."

"I'll call if I come up with something," Wendel said as he left before the Chief gave him another assignment.

"Not until Tuesday. Your murders have kept me so busy I'm taking my wife to Las Vegas for a couple days."

At home he wished Cheryl would call but found no messages on the answering machine. After a quick swim, he sat in her hot tub, trying to recall anything that might implicate her. In Burgher's office he thought she had asked how a thief might sell a stolen painting, supposedly information to help them identify and even locate the thief. Maybe she wanted the information for herself. Maybe she was out peddling the Klee right now. But that could hardly be the surprise she promised for Sunday. "Guess what. I stole your painting and sold it to a fence for a tenth of its value." After the tub, he threw on some clothes and made a peanut butter, lettuce, tomato and fried egg sandwich for lunch.

At a loss for how to pursue the murderer, who might be Cheryl, at least until she got home, he dabbed at the sandwich while trying out the GeTechNome experiment on line. Bored he hacked into the program as though he were out to steal GeTechNome secrets. Something looked different. It had been so late the other night at the company he hadn't downloaded their work onto a flash drive, so step by step he had to recall how they had left it. The change hit him almost as hard as finding Cheryl on Burgher's email the day before—someone had altered the program.

The change was subtle and camouflaged. Someone had inserted an exit. The exit path led to another camouflaged location that transcribed all the moves of people using the program. Dammit he thought—the company was into rudimentary tests and already security was shot.

Mad as he was, his energy lifted because now he had something to do. Find the intruder. Eight scientists had used the system since they set it up two days earlier. All eight had manipulated their tests, adding ingredients, reading their own results, siphoning off a mixture before adding additional ingredients. He couldn't trace the added routine to any of the eight.

The portals in and out of the added routine allowed the thief to log on, retrieve and log off. Wendel was pretty sure he could stand by and either identify or follow the intruder when he fetched the stolen information.

As happened when he became entrenched on line, Wendel lost track of time. When the telephone rang, he saw that dusk had settled around the house. Waldo Peterson barked into his ear, "Someone has broken into your system."

"Probably me, Waldo. I was checking it all afternoon." Low clouds were floating in from the ocean.

"Did you steal my data?"

"No."

"Someone has."

Wendel was surprised Peterson was so adept with computers, but then why shouldn't a world-class scientist in the twenty-first century be adept. Wendel reassured Peterson he was laying in wait to catch the intruder.

"Why don't I drop by so we can catch him together," Peterson said.

Wendel agreed. The more he could bring Peterson, critic-in-chief, into the process, the more other scientists would go along.

Wendel picked up a pizza in town and bought some Salmon for himself and Cheryl for the next night, hoping there might be an innocent explanation for Burgher's email to her. He opened a Pinot Grigio, and while he and Peterson ate the pizza in the kitchen, Wendel created a marinade in a frying pan to soak the salmon.

Upstairs at the computers—Peterson had brought his laptop—Peterson showed him work he had done and how he had detected the thief. He was damned good on line, good enough to catch the thief, or even be the thief,

Wendel thought. The two of them sat at Wendel's desk, trading computer stories. Peterson: How he had detected the intrusion into Wendel's program. Wendel: how he had found Cheryl on the Entwurf's September 7 email log.

"Try this on the Wurf's computer," Peterson said, as he fumbled through a list of programs on his laptop and emailed one to Wendel.

"Entwurf's."

"I wrote it one day when I was stumped on an experiment and needed a distraction."

Wendel hacked into the Entwurf's system and then Peterson took over. His program showed that the "September 7" email from Burgher to Cheryl had actually been placed by Burgher in Burgher's outbox on September 28, after he and Cheryl had been in Switzerland. Relief that Cheryl was not the thief or the killer ran through his mind and down through his body. But with that knowledge a chill followed his relief down his back.

"Burgher knows I used Cheryl's computer to get into the Entwurf system." He explained to Peterson how he had hacked into Burgher's system shortly after his vacation a month ago, that Burgher must have captured Cheryl's address at the time and then realized Wendel was the hacker when they were in his Swiss office a couple weeks ago. "Burgher must have inserted this email with Cheryl as recipient in lieu of the actual email. This means Burgher knows or will soon find out that I've hacked in again, that I'm investigating and am onto him. Maybe we shouldn't sit in front of this window."

Peterson said, "I know who the intruder is."

Wendel lit up and motioned him to go on.

"I confess that I put in the intercept."

"What?"

"I invaded the system at GeTechNome to see if it can be done. I wanted to see if you could stop me or even detect me."

Wendel sat back letting out a deep breath. "Okay, he said. A good challenge. I did detect you and damn right I can find you. Watch."

He tried to weave his knowledge of Peterson—brazen, creative, rebellious, even iconoclastic—with the forays into the system to work his way to Peterson's computer. Peterson pulled up a chair and watched, occasionally making a comment about Wendel's progress. "Cold," or "Getting warmer," or, "You're not as good as I thought," which pissed Wendel off and spurred him on.

A little before eleven Peterson filled Wendel's glass and said, "You are as good as I thought." Wendel knew he was close and keyed in the final two commands that led to the intruder. But the path did not lead to Peterson. It led to the Entwurf. He sipped the wine thinking through this result. When he lowered the glass, Peterson stood up, pointing a small caliber pistol at Wendel's head.

28

Fear and comprehension arrived together. Peterson was Handler's killer. As Wendel eyed the gun, he strained to keep his bowels from emptying. Peterson was going to kill him.

Peterson gestured for Wendel to swivel back to the computer and ordered him to execute a series of commands that wiped the work off the screen. The scientist handed Wendel a DVD, which he had Wendel insert. More commands erased the hard drive, overwrote all data.

"You won't be needing it," Peterson said.

"Why are you doing this?" Wendel asked.

"I'll tell you downstairs as long as you cooperate."

"Someone likely saw your car here," Wendel said over his shoulder as they headed down.

"I walked from my house," Peterson said.

"Your prints are all over my house."

"You invited me last week for your church. Besides I'm about to do the neighbors a favor and burn this place to the ground."

In the front hall Peterson said, "Stop here. I'm in no hurry if you really have the stomach to hear the story rather than get it over with."

Wendel's presence had returned. He'd been through this experience already this week. The Hammer had given him a dress rehearsal. He was totally calm. He'd probably die. Buy maybe he'd have an opportunity if he kept Peterson talking.

"Why should I be in a hurry," he said.

"You stumbled onto a coincidence when you returned from your vacation and discovered my email to Burgher on your computer. I shouldn't have sent the picture of the painting to him. By the way he doesn't have your painting and neither do I. I can't answer that mystery. Mr. Handler probably stole it after Burgher offered him five million."

"What's with you and Burgher?" Wendel said.

"I broke in here while you were gone to steal your computer work, to search your computer to learn how to avoid the security you were developing for GeTechNome. Unfortunately Mr. Handler returned and discovered me." Peterson's admission explained why the FBI thought Handler had searched Wendel's computer on the day of his murder—it had been Peterson, not Handler.

"So you killed Handler."

"I've been stealing GeTechNome's secrets for several years. I send them to Burgher who markets them to European biotech companies in exchange for a healthy reward. Burgher needs the money to feed his art hobby, and I'm tired of watching the capitalists like Frances Holmes, make the big money. When I saw that painting in your living room, I took a picture and emailed it to Burgher who knew where I was that night. His return email, that you found on his computer, was sent to me, not you, which was why you couldn't find it."

"And then you altered Burgher's email to make it look like the return went to my next-door neighbor whom Burgher met in Lucerne. What kind of game was that?"

"It was a game. We thought it was a good joke, but also a trap to see if you were still pursuing Burgher. I'm afraid your discovery sealed your death. Burgher wanted to kill you. I didn't. We agreed to use the email trick to find out if we needed to kill you. Unfortunately you flunked that test or passed it with flying colors, depending on how you look at it.

"That doesn't make sense," Wendel said. "What if someone else finds it and connects Burgher and Cheryl to the murders."

"You're right, which is why I'll delete the email at the entwurf." Wendel heard Peterson's ego and pride as the scientist gathered momentum with the story. Maybe Wendel could use the oversized ego to catch Peterson off balance long enough to give Wendel a chance.

"You're better with computers than I am," Wendel said.

"I never doubted that."

"I shouldn't have either. After all, you're a Nobel Laureate."

"I was afraid your work at GeTechNome would interfere with my access to other scientists' work. At first I took the lazy route and tried to kill the work-from-home project. Then I figured I could get all I need by breaking into your programs just as easily, maybe easier than sneaking around the labs at night. I'm getting too old for that."

What occurred next startled Wendel as much as Peterson. Just as Wendel was hoping, maybe even praying he hated to admit, for an earthquake, the patio door opened.

"I saw the light and figured you were up," Cheryl called out.

Peterson, with the first look of uncertainty Wendel had ever seen, turned for a moment toward the rear of the house. Wendel immediately grabbed Peterson's wrist as Peterson pulled the trigger. The shot angled through Wendel's shoulder and into the living room. Something hurt like hell but Wendel held on.

Peterson struggled to turn his arm back toward Wendel, while Wendel resisted with all of his strength. They were close enough to dance, maybe a foot apart, Wendel gripping Peterson's wrist, Wendel's blood on Peterson's shirt. Peterson's breath blew into his face, the smell of the garlic from the pizza.

Wendel struggled to create space to bring his left arm and hand into play to use the hand-to-hand combat maneuver he had learned in the army, and never again used. But the struggle with Peterson was not a one-motion maneuver like in practice. Peterson resisted and fired another shot that dug into the ceiling. Gradually Wendel pushed Peterson away enough to reach and grab his wrist with both hands. He twisted. The wrist didn't break, but Peterson could no longer hold onto the gun. For an instant it teetered with the trigger guard on his finger and fell to the floor. At that moment Cheryl crashed Wendel's only frying pan, the one with the marinating salmon, into the back of Peterson's head.

29

Sunday morning Wendel lay in bed next to Cheryl, enjoying a steady drizzle, punctuated with an occasional downpour. His shoulder, bandaged in the emergency room, throbbed but probably would function fairly well without surgery. He didn't want to do a thing—only enjoy his thoughts, which at the moment focused on what the hell had happened to the salmon after Cheryl swung the frying pan. He'd need another ozonator if he didn't remember to find it. They hadn't gotten to sleep until after four, second night in a row for Wendel, and he didn't expect Cheryl, who had been working late all week, to be up for quite a while. Quickly he answered the phone when it rang hoping it wouldn't awaken her. "Hold on," he whispered as he walked to the kitchen.

"I finally get away and you fuck up my vacation," the Chief said.

"Perfect timing. You didn't have to deal with the messy details."

"Okay, thank you. Spending half the night on the telephone with the LA police was better than driving back."

"Saved you all that money your wife won last night at the tables."

"Just wanted to tell you Peterson probably won't live, and if he does, he'll be a vegetable."

"You ought to save his brain for science," Wendel said.

"They won't learn much with what's left. Don't get into a fight with that girlfriend of yours. By the way, the Swiss arrested Burgher."

Wendel sat with a cup of coffee in a lounge chair on Cheryl's covered porch and watched rivulets of water wash down the dunes converging about where Cheryl's and his yards began. Recalling his fights with Margo years earlier produced anxiety over getting involved with Cheryl. Still he thought he was ready, at least to give it a try.

Intuitively Wendel knew he'd never be a rich man. The painting was surely gone, but he wouldn't know what to do with twenty-five million dollars even if weren't. He was meant to scratch along, enjoy the good fortune of having bought a valuable home years before, and lead a life with a healthy tension between what he had and what he needed. He preferred it that way.

Cheryl made a casserole for dinner and when she pulled it out of the oven, she said, "I'll make the decision on which wine goes best. Let's take a look."

Together they walked across his yard and climbed down into the bomb shelter that was even wetter than Friday. Cheryl chose "an expensive" Pinot Noir "that the occasion if not the meal warranted."

"Remember the surprise I mentioned," she said.

"Forgot all about it. Are you going to tell me?"

"Sit down. We have a few minutes before casserole's done. She retrieved a cork screw from the table drawer in the middle of the shelter and opened the wine. "Needs to breathe so we'll have to wait," she said.

"No hurry, except for the surprise. I'm on the edge of my seat."

"One night when Handler was here, I came over to invite him for a hot tub. I told you I might have heard Burgher and Handler talking, so I didn't walk in. Actually I listened. Burgher wanted to buy the painting. Handler said "no, not yet." I thought they were going to steal your painting, so the next day I let myself in and took it."

Excitement flooded Wendel, quickly followed by questions. The painting was saved. But why hadn't Cheryl told him? Why had she flown to Switzerland with him?

"I was fooling myself," Cheryl said. "I thought I was saving the painting for you, but then I realized I wanted the five million dollars. I wish it weren't true. I hate myself for having done this and didn't realize it until I spent the week on retreat."

She was crying now. Tears poured out in uncontrolled sobs. Wendel's first impulse was to hold her and reassure her, but feelings of betrayal held him back. She couldn't or wouldn't look at him, instead holding her head in her hands. Thoughts came next. How could she not have told him? All he had been through, yes because of the murders, but also the painting. Would they have gone to Switzerland had they known? But the Swiss trip had brought them together, made Wendel realize that maybe he wanted a close connection. Last night she had saved his life. How could he ignore that? But for Cheryl, Peterson would have shot him.

Cheryl brought out a handkerchief for her eyes. "I know it doesn't matter—" She couldn't go on. She choked back the words each time she tried to talk. After a moment she got down on her hands and knees and crawled toward the back of the shelter. Wendel thought about bending down and lifting her up. She didn't need to crawl in the mess of deteriorating concrete. But then she raised herself up, holding a roll of paper. The painting, Wendel thought. That was the surprise, the reason to fetch the wine. He did help her stand.

"Here," she said.

Wendel removed a rubber band, not sure if this was how to store a watercolor, and unrolled the scroll. Inside the paper was almost blank. A faint trace of scarlet remained as did the black lines, albeit faded and faint, but the water had washed away the images. Wendel's first reaction was to laugh. Twenty-five million dollars claimed by the surging ocean. Two murders had turned into a comedy. Only the screenwriter would have invented this ending. The washed-out page and Wendel's laughter silenced Cheryl. Then he realized that her betrayal was worse than the loss of the money.

30

In the back of his closet Wendel found a nice shirt to wear to the GeTechNome "coming-out" event for their work-from-home program. The governor would be attending as well as a host of environmentalists, public health officials, local dignitaries and CEOs from around the area whom Frances Holmes had invited with hopes they'd emulate her vision. He didn't even consider a necktie. Governor or no governor, this was California when it came to dress codes.

He still couldn't walk through the front hall without thinking back both to Handler and to the night Cheryl had wacked Peterson. After retrieving what was left of the painting in the bomb shelter, Cheryl and he had eaten Cheryl's casserole in silence. Neither of them could find the words for their feelings. Since then Cheryl had spent most of her weeks traveling, increasing her scheduled visits to wine shops and shopping-center promotions. Using the hot tub alone plunged Wendel into an even deeper funk than that evening had left him. He had already forgiven Cheryl, accepting her larceny as different scope but not morality from his own shenanigans of unauthorized "visits" to computer systems, visits he vowed to stop.

A beautiful November day allowed GeTechNome to hold its celebration outside. Wendel sat with the other guests listening to the speakers who stood in front of the building so that the golden reflective glass showed their backs, as though he were watching from inside. Several speakers mentioned Wendel for his contribution in developing a system that would keep employees' cars off the road several days a week and allow the business to continue somewhat normally in the event of quarantine during a public health crisis.

His mind was wandering through thoughts of the additional projects he would pick up from other companies when he heard his name. He looked up and saw Frances Holmes gesture his way. "Come on up, Wendel," she said. And as he walked forward, she added, "I wish I could show more respect, but our friend Wendel insists he has no first name and hates to be called mister."

"You saved our company," Frances said. He felt his face flush because even though he appreciated the recognition, he didn't know how to handle praise. He was about to say, "It was nothing," but knew that was silly. In fact he relished that the experience had taught him that his life and putting it at risk were not "nothing." So all he did was smile and after a few moments try to wave off the applause.

"In appreciation of your contribution to our existence," Frances continued, "we have a gift for you. Not that we haven't paid Wendel handsomely for his services," she added to the audience in a way that elicited laughs. From behind the dais she lifted a package, wrapped in brown paper, and handed it to Wendel. "Go ahead and open it," she said.

Wendel untied the string and removed the paper. For a moment he thought he was looking at a photograph, but then he realized that the surface of a photograph does not possess clumps of oil paint. He was holding one of the original Klee paintings that had hung outside Frances Holmes' office.

"We could never replace the unique watercolor you lost in your efforts for us. But we take great pleasure in giving you a distant second."

Over the weekend he insisted Cheryl come for dinner. "You can eat and run, but I want to show you something," he said.

On the wall of his living room he hung the washed-out page of the former watercolor. On one side he hung a photo of the watercolor and on the other the Klee that Frances had given him. Next to the photograph was the painting they had bought at Handler's gallery in Paris, the beginning of their collection Cheryl had said.

"I wanted you to see these," he said. "I'm returning the Klee to Frances Holmes on Monday. It has meaning to her, while the meaning for me is contained in this photograph, which is all that I ever thought I owned. I like keeping my doors unlocked, and I don't like having guards outside the house whom Frances hired until I install an elaborate security system. "

He stepped closer to Cheryl and put his arms around her, which she didn't resist. "Even more meaningful for me than the photograph is this faded painting. It represents so much that already exists between us and remains blank for us to decide how we want to fill in the rest of our lives."

The end.

Acknowledgments

I want to acknowledge special thanks to—

The Cambria Writers Group that does so much to foster fiction from the California Central Coast and my friends in the splinter writers group who listened to Drop Dead Art and provided suggestions and encouragement;

Judith Guest and Rebecca Hill of Inkwell Intensives who made learning to write a fun travel experience;

Anne Laddon who developed ideas about why my $3.00 photograph-poster of a supposed Paul Klee painting was probably from a painting created by someone other than Klee, and how that painting could have been an original watercolor;

Chris Clogston for explaining the keychain device that changes passwords every ten seconds;

Mark Grayson for motorcycle and survivalist tutorials;

Karesa Bullock, brainstormer of romantic touches;

Numerous biographers of Paul Klee whose books provided authority for the information included about Klee except for the fictional series of watercolors that the novel presents as having been painted late in Klee's life, whose existence I invented;

And mostly my poet-wife Jeanie who has played house with me for 35 years and who, along with her suggestions, mixes hugs, laughs and lots of love.